The Lord Otter

The Curse of the Star Wraiths
Steel & Stormbright, Vol. #1
Published by: Alcaron Publishing
Cover by: NeutronBoar
Map by: The Lord Otter
Illustrations by: NeutronBoar & UmbrellaKat
Special Thanks to: Inkarnate Pro

This book is a work of fiction. Names, characters, places, organizations, and events are either products of the author's imagination or used fictitiously. Any resemblance to actual events, places or persons, living or dead, is entirely coincidental.

First Edition, 2023

ISBN: 979-8-9892148-0-8

The Cost of Freedom

"I hope they're cheering for us," muttered Steel.

"You might want to listen closer," replied the ruffian, who until this point had remained silent. "They're shouting a name I've never heard before: 'Brugmar,' they cry, 'King of Beasts.'"

At some distance across there stood another portcullis. It opened with a similar screech of agony, a number of nearby fissures belching forth clouds of volcanic fumes, obscuring what lay beyond. The earthy smoke billowed as if it led to some abominable hellscape. The gladiators steadied themselves for what manner of creature might come—be it man, beast, or aberration.

At first there was a low rumble before footsteps shook the ground underneath. The crowd halted their cheers, a deathly silence falling over the entire arena.

A savage roar echoed from the darkness. A pair of yellow-slitted eyes pierced outward like rays of sickly light. The beast lumbered into view, its mottled patches of fur hiding no shortage of scars among its bulk. To the gladiators, it seemed like it shared aspects of man and beast: it stood at three times the height of those who opposed it, its face showing as a strange mix between lion and wolf. Its mane was wild and unkempt, and in one hand was held a massive battleaxe.

The creature grinned, displaying several rows of jagged teeth. Not unlike a shark.

Table of Contents

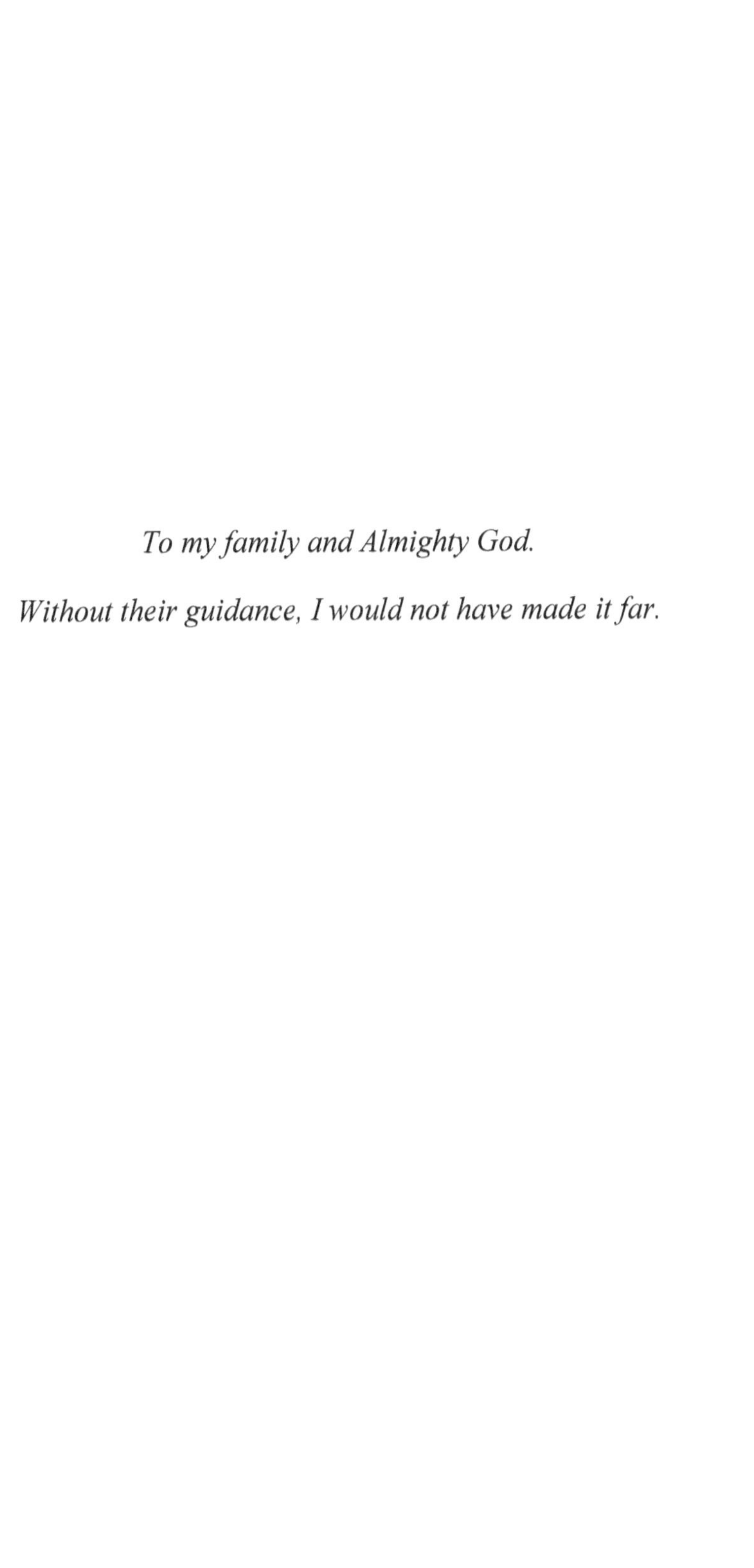

To my family and Almighty God.

Without their guidance, I would not have made it far.

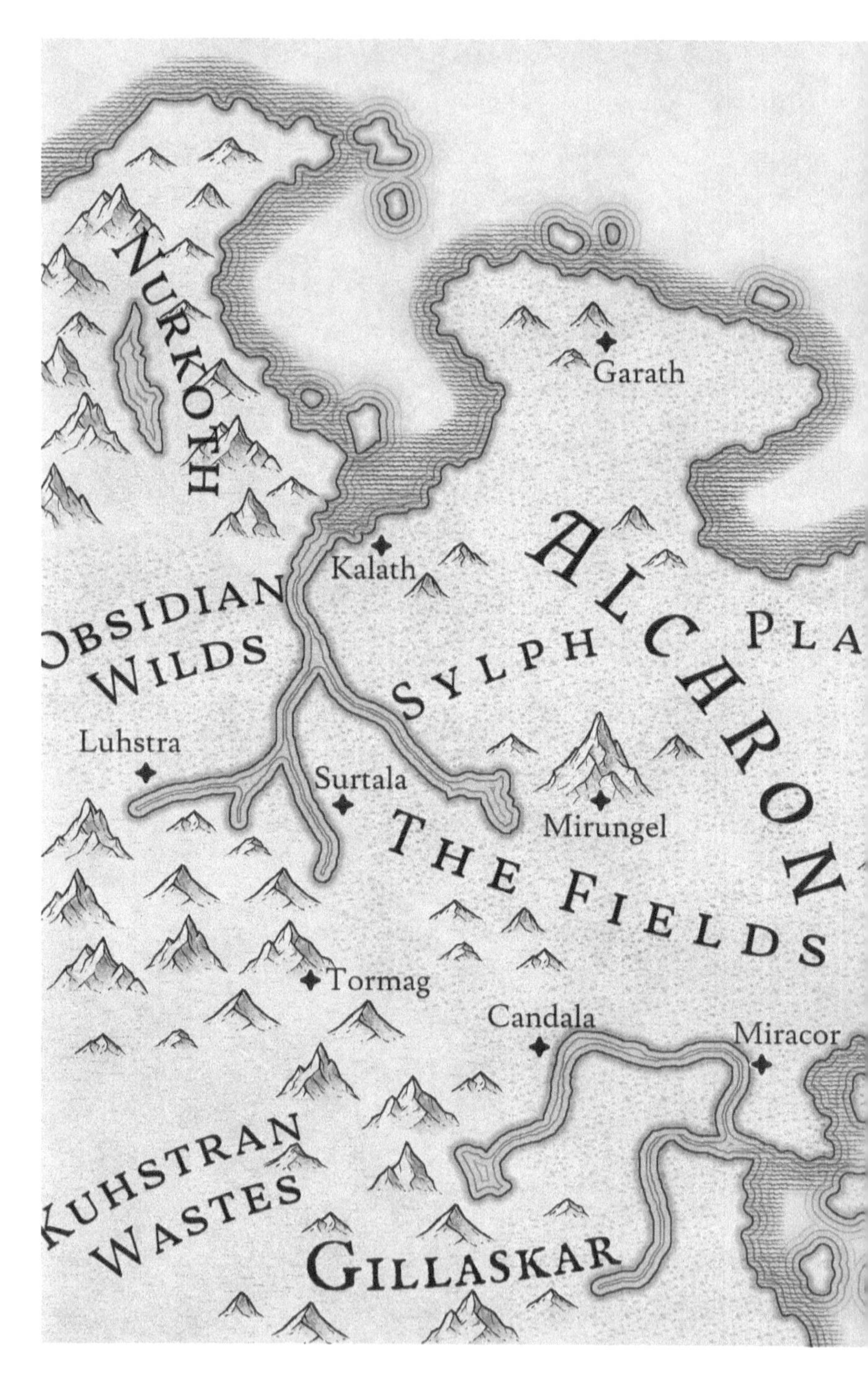

NURKOTH
OBSIDIAN WILDS
Kalath
Garath
ALCARON
SYLPH
PLA
Luhstra
Surtala
Mirungel
THE FIELDS
Tormag
Candala
Miracor
KUHSTRAN WASTES
GILLASKAR

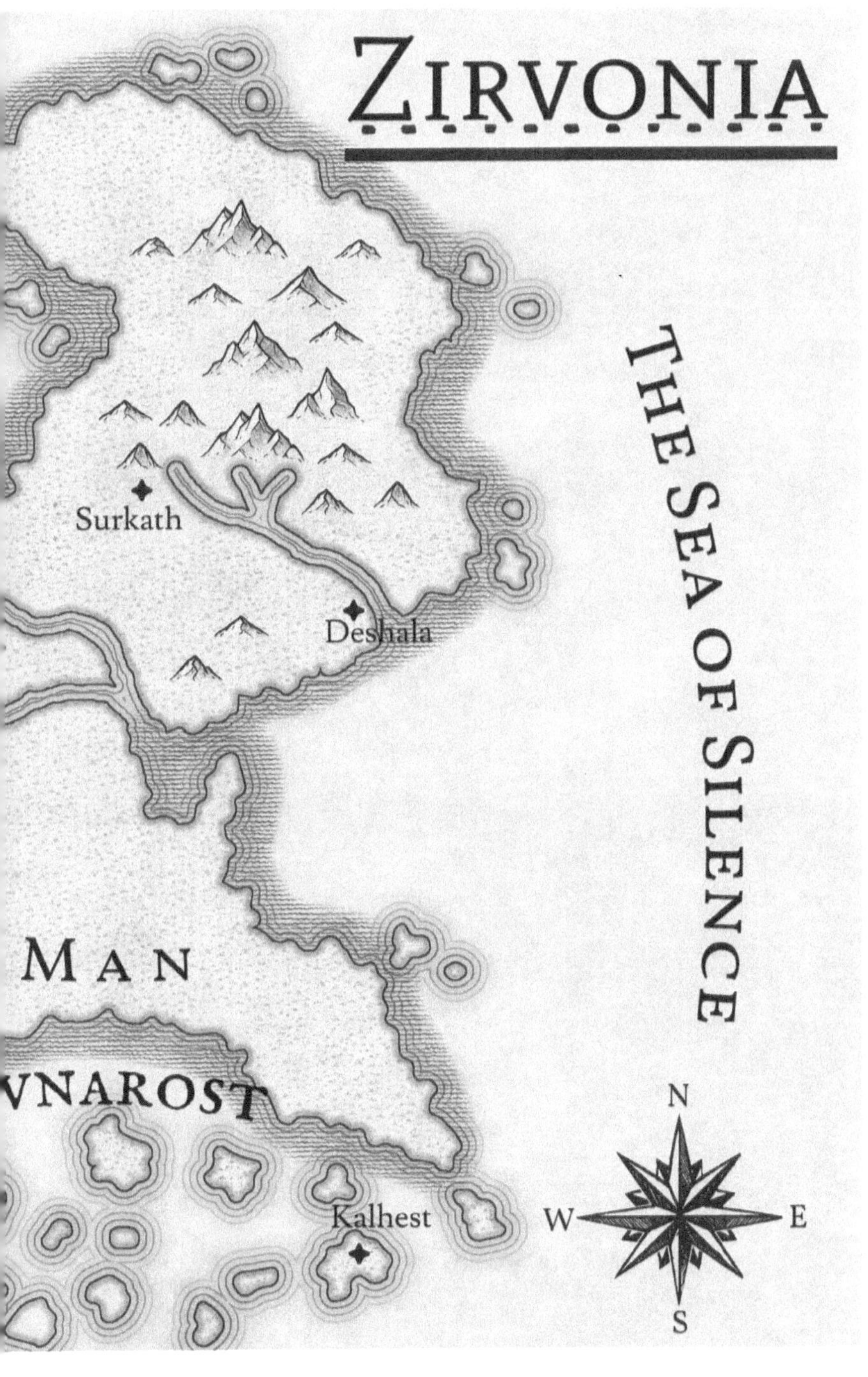

ZIRVONIA
THE SEA OF SILENCE
Surkath
Deshala
MAN
VNAROST
Kalhest
N
W
E
S

I
Origin

Darkness came in full as the storm clouds rolled overhead. The landscape reeled with its plains of golden grass, acacia trees, and cool rhododendrons dimming as if under a spell. All the magic and hope of that land vanished with it. In its place there came a feeling of ominous uncertainty, coupled with the odd streak of lightning.

The brothers frowned as they rode atop their mares. Their cowls spanned over their heads while rain soaked them to the bone. Normally Zolan and Serithas wouldn't have been surprised by weather like this. Yet it dawned on them that this was no ordinary storm; it arrived in a matter of minutes, and what started as a mild drizzle had become a downpour.

"It looks like we've chosen a bad time to visit mother's grave," said Zolan, his voice barely recognizable over the howling winds.

"Well it's too late to change that now," his brother replied. "This storm is getting worse by the minute. We should find some cover."

"Perhaps you're right." He looked about them, spotting a lone acacia tree standing nearby. Its branches swayed violently with the wind, yet it looked safer than the path they were riding along.

Lightning struck overhead.

Zolan's horse whinnied in response. The youth tried calming the beast, as he could feel her panicked movements coming from underneath him. He kept her calm enough so that she followed his brother. They departed from the path, and soon they were both underneath the boughs of the large acacia. The wind howled in their ears, though it seemed that the storm was steadily abating in intensity.

Serithas had dismounted when there came another flash of lightning, this time causing the tree over them to erupt in a plume of flames. The two horses reeled in panic as they sped off in opposite directions. Serithas cried out in shock, seeing that his brother was carried away by his mare. It was only a short moment before they were separated, the downpour drowning out their shouts for one another.

The rain pounded against his face. Following several attempts to rein in his mount, Zolan pulled back with all his strength. At first it seemed that the beast might stop then and there before she turned. He felt himself leave the saddle; his hands groped along for any kind of hold, yet it was too late as he landed in the mud with a crash!

He lay there for some time before his senses returned—how long he wasn't sure. Eventually, his eyes opened as he struggled to his feet. Despite all his efforts to move both arms he could only do so with his left. The other felt as if it had been thrust over a fire, each movement coming with a horrific jolt of pain.

It was obvious that his shoulder had been dislocated…

He was also alone.

"Serithas! Serithas!" he cried. There was no response.

His eyes welled up with tears as he stumbled along the nearest hillside. In truth, being a boy of thirteen years, Zolan was largely scorned by his peers for acting too much like a child. He had relied on his older brother for so much. This fact was made all the more evident when he had been forced to hunt a prized elk on his own, returning several hours later with nothing to show for it. He was too weak—his elders said as much.

He continued to weep in frustration. Though only a couple years spanned between them, Serithas had always appeared so fearless and confident. Now the thought of being left alone was an utterly terrifying one.

Somehow he would have to fend for himself. He would have to survive.

The lad stifled his emotions, coming face-to-face with a large boulder. Unfortunately its surface was too smooth to serve as any real cover. Zolan had thought of another use for it.

He steadied his breathing and tried remaining calm, though in reality his heart was racing. Thankfully he had seen Harskul's shaman treating injuries like this before. At least enough to know how to deal with it. The winds were shy of being a fully-fledged cyclone, and there was no guarantee that Serithas was even alive.

He would have to find his brother, and that likely meant having full use of both arms.

Thus he twisted his shoulder and slammed it against the stone. He felt the joint being popped into place, though that didn't stop him from roaring out in pain.

Zolan dropped to his knees, retching as his mind wavered along the edge of consciousness. His heartbeat steadied as both the agony and adrenaline subsided. He was so tired… but he would have to move on if he hoped to survive.

That was when he heard his name being called out among that storm.

At first he thought it was Serithas who found him. Zolan smiled in relief, moving to the hill's summit to try and survey his surroundings…

No one was there.

"*Zolan*," the voice spoke out again. Only this time it appeared to come from the heavens themselves.

The youth became frightened. How could he hear his own name being spoken if it wasn't his brother? It couldn't have been the other men of Harskul. They were too far away for anyone to find them. The weather was too violent. So who was this other person who called out to him?

That was when he saw it. Out from the rain and wind there emerged a figure who towered high over everything else. Though it was human-like in appearance, its eyes glowed with a thunderous, supernatural fury. Each stride resounded like a thunderclap, a long mane waving independent of its surroundings.

Zolan trembled where he stood, realizing that this figure must have been some sort of deity. Of course, he had heard tales of men speaking with gods from before; but he never thought that *he* would be the one to have such an encounter.

Calamtu, he thought. Yes… it had been their shaman who told him stories of this deity. Like most of the other gods who dwelled in this world, the master of storms was said to be unpredictable in His behavior. One could be reduced to cinders just as they might

"That was when he saw it."

be given His blessing. Calamtu was known as a god of might, one who wrought terrible destruction for all who stood in His path.

Zolan couldn't believe himself. This storm was *His* doing!

The figure halted in stride—standing over the boy as if it were a massive statue. He wasn't sure what this being could have wanted with him, yet he was almost certain it was outside his understanding. Every fiber of his being quaked in fear—but there was also some part of him that waited with anticipation.

That was when a hand twice his size moved over him. From those massive fingers there danced blue streams of lightning. Deep within his soul, Zolan felt something similar stir and awaken— something which *responded* to that stimulus.

He realized that the lightning was coming from himself. His eyes began glowing as well, and his voice didn't waver as he spoke, almost as if in declaration.

"Stormbright."

The giant smiled as He lifted His hand. Another flash of lightning came forth as it blinded the youth. By the time his sight had returned, all signs of the deity were gone.

It wasn't long after that Zolan lost consciousness, the energy dispersing as his body fell to the scorched earth. It would be several hours later before he was found by Serithas. Even in the days following their return, he would recall little from their time being separated. There would be no memory of what transpired after falling from his horse, nor of the god he had encountered within that storm.

In the wake of destruction, the Fields of Man were largely spared. Only the odd scorch mark and fallen branch indicated that the land had been changed at all. There remained an unnatural silence, a sense of unrest which hushed the sighs between blades of grass—even the rustling of leaves among the trees and bushes.

Following some time, the disquiet broke as the cavalcade of soldiers made their march. The light of the sun reflected off their helms and cuirasses, forged of brass and shimmering moonsteel. Their arrayment of skewers bobbed up and down in unison. Their symmetrically perfect faces looked on without wavering, being toned a light shade of bronze.

To the common passerby, their presence might have appeared divine or even angelic, as their knotted arms and thews bent under the weight of their armor. Not a single person faltered in stride; not one made a step out of line.

At the front of this Ilgrathian squadron were two figures. The first settled upon her gelding, swaying imperceptibly whilst staring forward. She wore no helm—her mane of golden hair tied back in a single braid which curled along her shoulders.

Meanwhile, the human beside her was a solid cubit shorter. He was hooded and wiry of figure, and everything down to his ebony hair and melancholic mannerism showed that he was nothing like his superior. His robes were a dismal black, and his face was gaunt and worn out by untold years of obedience.

This sorcerer, whose name was Aedas, moved his eyes over to his companion; the Falconer cast him a passing glance.

"Keep your eyes to yourself," she commanded. "I don't enjoy it when one of your kind looks at me that way."

The man obeyed without question.

"We still have a job to do, and you know your role in it." Her eyes returned to their surroundings. "I believe we should be close enough now."

They stopped by the trail. Here it seemed that the storm's destruction had been at its worst. Whole sections of the land were overturned, and nearby was an acacia that had been burned to cinders. A series of scorch marks littered the area, which was undoubtedly caused by several lightning strikes in one place.

"Strange," she said. "This seems like a good place to start, if any." They rode a short distance before she turned to her companion, her voice hardening as if she were commanding a slave. "Astromancer, begin your scrying. This area seems most suspicious."

Aedas was quick to respond, his eyes clouding a milky white as he dismounted. For a second his hands moved as if they were gripped by a palsy; his mind traveled along past, present, and future. He could see everything that had transpired there, everything which might also happen. But it was always difficult to discern the finer details. Faces, in particular, were a haze to his mind—even for one so experienced as he—yet he could at least divine the broader strokes of what had happened.

"Yes, I can see it," he spoke absently. "A sorcerer was here not long ago. It seems as if his powers were awakened by some being or god. I do not know what it was exactly, but I can tell that it has caused this destruction." He gestured around them as his concentration lapsed, his senses briefly overwhelmed. His eyes cleared of that mysterious magic.

"How long ago was this?" General Caerst inquired.

"A little over three weeks," he said. "The magician couldn't have gone far. He was weak, and anyone whose sorceries are awakened will require time to adjust."

"And did you see his face?"

The astromancer shook his head.

She sighed. "No wonder the others speak your name with such high praise. For a human, at least, your magic is quick and you get straight to the point."

"Truly, I am honored." He bowed before remounting his horse. He was not sure why exactly, but he had omitted the fact that their target was joined by another—likely they were friends or brothers by his own conjecture?

He waved away the thought. They rode onward for a time as Aedas mustered the courage to speak.

"If I may ask, how did you learn of this anomaly?"

General Caerst frowned at him. "It was found out by Ilgrathié," she said with a hint of reluctance. "Apparently, this magic was so powerful that even She took notice. There was no other reason given, only that we should find any sorcerers responsible and deal with them."

"It sounds like She is afraid," he said.

"*Watch* your words." A moment passed before she continued, her tone becoming a tinge more even-measured. "This sorcerer could complicate things for us. Right now it is vital that we expand our borders, and we can't afford to have any rogue magicians working against us." She looked at him again, this time with more menace. "Is that understood, Aedas?"

He nodded while going silent, wordlessly cursing his fate. Why had the goddess chosen him for a task like this? Surely, She must have realized his connection to the area. Most humans came from the Fields of Man, after all, and what was more, he had recognized these parts as home.

That had been decades ago. Only then it was Aedas and his brother, along with Maelith, the woman he had loved so dearly.

He could still recall the day when the Ilgrathians invaded, conquering the Fields of Man under one fell swoop. His fellow men had fought valiantly, though there was little defense against the Almari—those Ilgrathian soldiers who rode on the backs of giant birds. Several cities were razed in a matter of hours, and somehow he and his brother were separated. Maelith was also taken from his arms that day, where he was forced to witness her rape and murder.

Thinking about it now, his only means of survival had come through his predisposition for magic. It was required that his mind be broken to prevent any thoughts of rebellion. The Ilgrathians had beaten him so many times, tortured his mind and body to where they were but fragments of a greater whole. He hated them for it—despised them, in fact. But there was a part of him that kept in line, staying loyal to his sadistic masters.

They were nearing their destination. Already the landscape was becoming more familiar by the second. Aedas could see a faint trail leading up ahead, snaking by a close escarpment before arriving at a collection of animal-shaped huts.

Bloodshed was soon to follow.

When the Ilgrathians arrived, the villagers of Harskul were struck with immediate fear. There was no place for them to go— nowhere to flee from those terrifying soldiers. Their adversaries had come without warning, and despite the village being almost hidden to the naked eye, there was little they could do with the enemy at their doorstep.

The soldiers gleamed fiercely as they stood in formation, appearing like figures out of legend. To Serithas, he knew what these people were capable of, and his fear held him firmly in place while standing amongst the crowd.

It had been several weeks since he had returned with his brother, and though Zolan was fast on the road to recovery, he was still somewhat weak from their excursion.

The two mounted figures stopped at the edge of the village. One was slim and beautiful, her plated armor making little noise as she dismounted. Beside her the man in robes did the same.

The woman's eyes swept from side-to-side, her aquiline features giving her a likeness to a bird of prey.

"I'm pleased that our entrance has not gone unnoticed," she said sardonically. "My name is General Caerst. I am a Falconer of Ilgrathié, and I come here on urgent business. There are reports that a rogue magician is hiding in the area, and we have reason to believe he is here among you."

A sharp whisper spread throughout the crowd. Even in their small corner of the world, they had heard tell of how these Falconers—these first-born Ilgrathian women—were chosen at a young age, taken and given a drop of their goddess' blood. It was well-known that this enhanced their abilities, increasing both their strength and cunning, while doing little to change their bodily appearance. It was the greatest gift a warrior goddess could give her pupils, as their tales of bloodletting and conquest were legendary.

It was then that two of the villagers stepped forward. One was burly and not unlike a giant, his auburn hair falling behind his powerful shoulders, as a claymore was strapped to his back. In contrast, the man beside him was exceedingly small and frail. His bald pate reflected the light of the sun, and though his voice was haggard, there was a musical eloquence as he spoke.

"I bid you welcome, General Caerst. My name is Gulizar, and I am the shaman of Harskul. I must admit, we haven't found any signs of a sorcerer around these parts. Tell us, what information has given you such an idea?"

The general frowned. "My companion here has informed me that a human was awakened. I am told this person is nearby, assuming his visions are accurate."

"So you've an astromancer with you. Truly, General, this seems insincere coming from an order which eschews magic—using one sorcerer to track another, that is."

The Falconer spoke in between her teeth. "You are testing my patience."

"The feeling is mutual. Have your sorcerer cast his spells and begone! We have nothing to hide from you, and you can rest assured that there's no magician hiding among us."

Her temper boiling over, she gestured to Aedas. The man hesitated as he witnessed the shaman's stern expression. Serithas sensed that there was some connection between the two, as if something were being conveyed from one man to the other.

All of that vanished, however, when Aedas looked away and began moving his hands, a milky white film enveloping his eyes.

His other movements became imperceptible, as if his energy were being refocused into weaving that magic.

"He is here," he said after a moment.

"Well, which one is he?"

"I-I do not know."

General Caerst gave him a wary look. Her hand hovered over the pommel of her rapier. "Then we do it my way," she said. "Search them, my soldiers, bring anyone here who seems suspicious."

The soldiers marched forward without hesitation, filtering through the crowd with frightening speed. A few screams

emerged, yet they were quickly silenced as blades were drawn, held against the necks of those captive villagers.

"You cannot do this!" shouted the giant, drawing his claymore. "We have done nothing against you!"

"Oh, that remains to be seen," she replied. "In fact, let's bring you for inspection first."

Two soldiers locked their grip around his arms. The burly warrior tried resisting, yet their combined strength was greater. They brought him a fair distance closer, where he was forced to his knees in submission.

"My, you are a strong one." Her eyes narrowed. "Tell me— what is your name, human?"

"Kolthan," he growled in reply.

"Well, Kolthan, you seem like one who doesn't break easily under pressure. That is good. Sorcerer or not—you shall make a fine example for the others."

One of the soldiers stepped along his right flank, a spear poised to strike. Kolthan didn't hesitate as he wrestled away one of his hands with a jerk, using it to pull down the Ilgrathian on his left. The squirming soldier fell, acting as a shield against the weapon that struck downward. A scream erupted, the soldier going still in an instant.

Before the other Ilgrathian could react, Kolthan swung upward with his fist. It connected with the man's jaw, bringing him right off his feet. A whimpering followed as it was clear the bone had been broken.

Now rising himself, Kolthan brandished his enemy's spear, his flowing hair half-obscuring his face. He raised it while diving forward, charging past the flanking soldiers towards General Caerst. Any lesser veteran would have been slain then and there, but Kolthan barreled through his enemies as if they were nothing at all.

"Do not think you have won, wench! I shall never relent in the face of evil. Not ever!"

General Caerst did not falter. Unsheathing her rapier, she formed a lithe, defensive stance, anticipating which move her opponent might make. The giant reared up his weapon before feinting to one side. His stab was true, being aimed straight at her heart…

He would have succeeded had she not sidestepped, cleaving off his one arm near the elbow, before delivering another cut along his back.

The giant yowled as he fell face down. He tried moving up from where he lay but found that he couldn't. The cut at his back was simply too deep, almost enough to paralyze him.

The Falconer held her weapon at his neck. Her expression was one of mockery as she spoke, "Like I said, you make the perfect example."

Her actions didn't go unnoticed. Serithas had inched his way closer during the fight. He was near enough, and he couldn't stand to see his father humiliated any longer.

He made his move. Drawing a hunting dagger, he dashed in between his foes, shouting with violent rage as he trained it towards her throat.

"No! Serithas!" he heard his father cry out. But it did not matter to him. He would rather see this Falconer cast into oblivion for her crimes. She was a demon made manifest!

She moved just in time—enough so that his dagger glanced off her breastplate. "You little shit!" With a swift movement, she grabbed and twisted his one arm behind his back. A tremor shook his entire frame as his muscles locked in place, the blade wrenched from his hand and cast aside.

Serithas realized that any movement was futile. Pain shot through his nerves as General Caerst's rapier pressed against his neck. The woman's grip was like iron; he knew instinctively that any unwanted movement would see his throat sliced open. He could do nothing, save for scream as the agony spread along his nerves.

"So you recognize this child?" The Falconer grinned. "Standing here, I can see the resemblance between father and son. Two fiery souls—both misguided, but strong all the same!"

"Please," Kolthan begged. "I surrender. You may do whatever you like with me, but please spare my boy."

A long pause followed before another voice interjected. "Enough! I will not see my people brought through this torture any longer. It is I who conjured this magic you speak of. I am your magician—I, Gulizar!"

At this Caerst frowned. "That remains to be seen, Shaman." She turned to her companion. "Aedas—see if the man is speaking the truth."

As commanded, the astromancer moved forward. His hands passed along the human's features, his eyes going white as he traversed the boundaries between time and space.

Even before the spell was completed, Aedas knew his answer.

"The man speaks the truth," he said. "We've found our magician, General."

"Good! Bring him here!"

Serithas was released and thrown to the ground. His head spun as his muscles ached with fire, his body reeling from the pain he had endured. After a moment his senses recovered, and he motioned himself closer to his father. He tore a strip of cloth from his own tunic, binding Kolthan's arm stump as best he could.

Next to Serithas the shaman was brought forth, a knee from his captors bringing him to his haunches. "Do you have any last words, Shaman, before you go and meet your heathen gods?"

Gulizar smiled as he cast a look towards the youth. There was something in his expression, as if the shaman knew something that Serithas didn't.

He faced General Caerst. "Only that your fate will be the same as ours. I have seen what your goddess is capable of, and I can tell you that She is nothing but a heathen Herself. Come the end, only *you* will be left to sift through the pieces of that empire you hold so dearly."

"The prophecy of a fool," she said. Holding aloft her rapier, she slashed downward and the deed was done. The shaman's body slumped to the ground. His smile was no less apparent as his head rolled along her feet.

She wiped her blade with a kerchief, turning to the soldiers at her side. Her voice was like ice as she muttered the horrific words.

"Burn the village. We take the rest as slaves."

"No!" Kolthan cried, though it was too late to resist. The soldiers of Alcaron were already moving, their torches setting fire to everything surrounding those stone huts. The warriors of Harskul fought for both their lives and families. However, their strength paled in comparison to their captors.

They were cut down in an instant. The smoke stained the huts— those glaring animal faces—all the while the villagers were pulled out screaming, beaten and humiliated, bound in chains.

"Serithas," Kolthan whispered, "take your brother and flee this place. You cannot let yourselves be caught, no matter what."

"But father, I-" Tears were running down his face.

"There is no time! You must go… now!"

The boy nodded as he fled the hands of his captors, bolting within the crowd like a shadow. It was soon after that Kolthan tried moving, but not before a metal boot planted itself in his back.

"He won't make it far," said General Caerst. "But I love to see them squirm."

Serithas dove into the shelter of his hut. Thankfully, theirs hadn't been set on fire just yet. Zolan was lying there asleep, as he was still weak from his mysterious condition. "Wake up, Zolan! We have to leave—now!"

"Serithas… what is happening outside?"

That was when he felt a blade being held against his back. Serithas turned in dismay, spotting the Ilgrathian who stood beside him.

"Just one more move, child, and that's the last thing you'll ever say."

The sound of chains rang clear as their wrists were bound, both brothers led outside. Already the others were gathered into two columns, their moans and cries magnified as the harsh sound of the whip was announced.

So began their lives as slaves.

II

The Gates of Paradise

The lands went silent while the slaves plodded alongside their captors, their numbers dwindling through a mixture of grief and exhaustion. Aedas rode beside his superior, his expression a solemn one, as he was sorely overcome with guilt for what he had done.

General Caerst did not cease in her march. Nor did her men who lingered a short distance behind. They traveled without halting for several days, only gathering rest when fatigue assailed the strongest of their number. This was typical for Falconers, as they were encouraged to bring the strongest of slaves for their cause.

Thus a line was drawn for the sickly and weak. Their bodies were left unshackled, scattered along either side of the road for the carrion birds to feed. It was a most grisly scene to look upon, and the astromancer's stomach twisted with each passing second.

Dusk fell without warning, with firewood being gathered for the Ilgrathians who pitched camp. The sun's final rays peaked over the horizon before subsiding. Night followed, and Zirvonia's twin-moons could be spotted crossing overhead. Bruann, the first of the two, yawned in full crimson splendor while Taldriath emitted its violet hues, the latter a short distance farther out among the skies.

Often, Aedas pondered these celestial bodies as they coursed along opposite paths. It was said by the first astromancers—those wisest of the Islirian race—that one day the moons would eventually collide. Of course, this was never seen as a reliable prediction; it had come before their own curse and subsequent downfall. A vast oversight in predicting the future, as seen by many. Still, Aedas always held to the idea that *something* might disrupt the world from its current, wretched course.

It was a mere hope.

The fields, meanwhile, appeared like they were bathed under a thick coating of blood. It was in that sanguine light that the soldiers passed out scraps of food to their captives. Those who lived ate voraciously, including the giant and his two sons.

The astromancer turned his gaze back to his superior. General Caerst was sitting atop a lone hillock, eyeing her slaves and soldiers with the utmost scrutiny. Even now, he could sense her hatred, her unwavering fanaticism towards their cause…

It was a good thing the hatred was mutual.

Next morning peeked over the horizon as they reached their destination. Their march continued without stopping through those golden, swaying fields. The sun rose steadily, which caused the air around them to radiate with sweltering heat.

Now passing over a mound which housed a pavilion on one side, the Ilgrathians found that they were once again at the edge of Paradise.

It wasn't a lie that they had looked upon that vista many times before. Mirungel, or the City of Chimes, as it was called. However, it never failed in stealing their breaths away.

The path continued a short way further before reaching the base of a solitary mountain. Circling around it were several belts of gardens and pavilions not unlike the one next to them. A number of orchards lay about as well, the vegetation appearing to take on a more vibrant and colorful hue.

There was also the sounding of musical instruments, coupled with birds flocking from miles all around. They coursed whimsically around clusters of spires, minarets, and turrets; all as a massive structure gleamed at the mountain's summit.

General Caerst smiled. Aedas frowned in turn.

Venturing closer, they were met with the sight of ivory walls, along with two massive doors forged of gilded brass. They were granted passage and cheered on by crowds of onlookers lining the streets. It was the Falconers who held such a great measure of respect among their people; and though this had been a minor skirmish, in truth, the defeated slaves bolstered the city-goers' morale. For their belief was strong that the world had been wrought by heathen gods, and that Ilgrathié would save it from damnation.

As such, all other races were considered impure and lesser, as they hadn't descended from the same bloodline as their goddess. Still, there would be *some use* for these lower beings, even if they couldn't join their masters in Paradise.

So it was that the people of the streets sang with admiration. Dozens of faces peered on from above, their minds aloof as they indulged in bodily pleasure—from drugged wines, to inhaled narcotics, even their sex-slaves.

Past them all, the city of Mirungel spanned upward along an assortment of ramps and terraces, all of them decorated with hanging gardens and artificial streams. The soldiers ventured up one of these paths, with sweet-smelling flowers cast down on their heads and shoulders. The slaves' treatment was less favorable, as the odd bit of rotten fruit or feces was flung in their direction. The projectiles bruised and brought about several scratches, though otherwise they remained unmolested.

They came to another pair of doors, though these were scarcely a quarter height of what they had passed through before. The entrance was carved at the face of a lofty escarpment, its features oddly blank and ominous.

Two guards stood at either side. They cast the Falconer a concerned look as she dismounted.

"I come with new slaves in tow," she announced. "Please take them below the city with full haste. As for this one," she indicated towards Kolthan, "he is to be separated from the rest and brought to the Soul Cistern. There he should provide some use to our cause—if not in life, then perhaps so in death."

"As you command," replied the guard on her left, both of them bowing in turn. He vanished behind the doors, before reemerging with a dozen more in number. They stepped forward, seizing the slaves with a violent grip. Aedas kept his head bowed as he followed General Caerst and the other soldiers away from the struggle. He couldn't bear to look on that dismal scene, nor hear the shouts and cries of those he had wronged.

It was shortly past noon when the soldiers disbanded, leaving Aedas and General Caerst with one final task before the day's end.

They led their horses away from the ivory barracks, passing underneath a portcullis. Both could tell the air was thinning from whence they rode. Such occurrences weren't uncommon in a city like Mirungel, and so the prospect bothered them little. Before them snaked a white road which led over a series of ramps and stairs, along with many noble estates. Eventually they came to the summit that Aedas had spotted a short time earlier. Along its walls of pearl-white stone and gilded brass there patrolled a number of guards.

"I come to deliver my report to Her Radiance," spoke the Falconer, addressing the Ilgrathian who manned the gate. Aedas remained still atop his mount.

"As you wish," the other nodded, as if this were little more than routine business. "I can tell that Ilgrathié wishes to speak with you directly on the matter. Please follow me."

The guard was joined by another as they led General Caerst and Aedas through the adjacent hall. Even to experienced veterans like themselves, the heavenly sights and sounds struck deep to their core. They emanated the essence of power—pain and pleasure—those radiant halls of gold!

The effect was most entrancing to the senses, and it seemed they were walking along a dream of unending delights.

They scaled a mighty staircase before emerging outside. A narrow bridge spanned over a wide and deep chasm. The guards and their guests moved carefully across, as there wasn't any railing to rely on. The guards stationed themselves along the opposite side, with General Caerst and Aedas being ordered to continue walking.

A man in robes greeted them as they paced along a winding series of corridors. Many paths were open for them to take, but their guide didn't show any signs of doubt, as several men had memorized entire sections of that maze.

They were passed off from one robed figure to another. It was after several minutes of wandering that they reached a small antechamber.

"Our path ends here," murmured the guide, his soft voice magnified by the lofty room of white stone and metal decorations. He stood to one side as a large doorway loomed before them.

General Caerst turned to her companion. "I believe we shouldn't keep Her Radiance waiting any longer." She opened the doors, a brilliant light bathing her features. Inside, it was as if the idea of ecstasy was made manifest, the golden air providing supplication to one's spirit. The massive chamber was lined on either side with a series of columns, the width of each being five-cubits in diameter.

A red carpet led up a series of steps, halting at the feet of a lavish divan. Every conceivable design was inlaid on its surface. Along it stretched a number of slaves, all naked of garment though well-fed. They were men and women both—some splayed in a lazy and drugged manner as others stood nearby, their hands propping up trays full of wine and viands.

Ilgrathié lounged among them, her supple frame shimmering forth a vibrant, golden aura. General Caerst averted her eyes as she knelt beside Aedas, the latter bowing so deeply that his forehead touched the marble floor. She could tell that her goddess was incredibly beautiful—so much so that the prospect of gazing at Her directly was enough to instill mortal fear.

A sonorous voice spoke to her, the words resounding in a stark vibrato.

"So, one of my children has returned," She mused. "Tell me, O Caerst, what news do you bring from your excursions to the south? Has our little threat been quelled? Is there aught that I should be informed of?"

"It has, Your Radiance," replied General Caerst. The golden lights danced and curled about her feet. She could not help but tremble as she continued. "Through the efforts of my men and I, we traced this anomaly to a nearby village. Harskul was its name, and it was there that we found our sorcerer."

So she recounted all they had done, noting that the anomaly had arrived as a violent thunderstorm. She spoke of the rogue magician and how he hid after being awakened. Though they met resistance in the form of Kolthan and a few other warriors, the humans were no problem for their fighting prowess.

"This warrior chief, Kolthan, dared to threaten my life and reputation," she said. "I saw it fit to give him special punishment, a perfect example for the others."

An aura of despair came from the goddess. The halls darkened about them ever so slightly, and though she dared not look up, it seemed that Ilgrathié shook her head in disapproval.

"And so you brought him to the Soul Cistern," was the goddess' reply, "the place where the strongest spirits are taken and broken. It's not an unbefitting punishment, General; however the place isn't some torture chamber to be used on a whim. We must be certain that our prisoners are properly conditioned before extraction. Otherwise, we risk an uprising on our hands."

"I-I did not consider that," the Falconer stammered.

The goddess remained silent as the chamber went cold. General Caerst swallowed nervously. The Falconers were encouraged to discipline those who resisted, yet the punishments themselves were made in the Slave Pits. By contrast, the Soul Cistern had been constructed for another purpose. There the odd prisoner would be led into its gloomy depths, his soul drained in an instant for some greater, unknown purpose. Apparently its use was vital to the city at large, as only slaves with promising souls were deemed worthy.

Or so she had been told. She didn't know the real reason for its existence. Only that she had used it as a plaything to stroke her ego.

"Your ambition runs strong," continued Ilgrathié, "but try not to let pride cloud your judgment." With a hint of reluctance, the light resumed its heavenly warmth. "Very well, General. If that is the punishment you have decided, then I will allow it but this once. It seems he would have qualified for the extraction process anyway. However, I would caution you before repeating such a mistake, for it is not your place to gallivant with such devices. You must leave *that* to the sciomancers.

"But come—this isn't the time for harsh words. You have achieved much these last few weeks. And as reward for your actions, I shall see to it that your next duty is of great importance. The invasion to the south draws closer with each second, and I would see that you lead the charge. The Islirians are a formidable enemy, General, though I doubt they would hinder one such as yourself."

General Caerst lifted her head slightly. The realization hit her that she wasn't being punished at all. Instead she was being promoted.

"It wouldn't at all, Your Radiance," she replied.

Ilgrathié continued: "Even from here, I can tell that it's your wish to prove yourself. I can see the glimmer of it in your eye, the same fire which fuels your heart and resolve. It is why I entrust this war to you, General. See that I'm not mistaken in my judgment."

"Your Radiance," she stammered, "I stake my very life upon it. Should I fail, then you may do with me what you wish. Only then will I know that life is without purpose."

The figure nodded. "It is settled then. Rest assured that your efforts will benefit us more than you can imagine. Upon our victory here, we shall have dealt a grievous blow to our enemies. The other kingdoms will shudder upon hearing our names, and fear will gnaw at their hearts before our blades are drawn against them!"

"Indeed!" spoke General Caerst, her passion taking full hold of her.

"But first, I should inform you of the advantage our enemy holds. The Islirians are the first astromancers to walk this realm, and rest assured that they are the most powerful. Not only this, but their knack for magic is unequaled. This has made their defenses strong from what my spies have told me, though I hold fast that they won't stand long against our soldiers."

"If I may ask," the Falconer interjected, "what would we gain by invading these Islirians? They are but a shadow of their former selves. There is also this curse I've heard of, where each of them is said to turn into wraiths after dying. Shouldn't we let them perish first, then swarm in and take what's left?"

"A good question," replied the goddess. "The Islirians have lived for sometime now under their curse, and if I am to guess, they've probably found a means of warding off their more sinister selves. Still, it's important to know what we can do with this technology of theirs. It is rumored that at one point they ruled the skies with flying ships. Just imagine how this might help us in liberating the rest of the world!"

"I see," she murmured. "It shall be yours, Your Radiance."

"Then you are aware of the importance of your role, and all that it pertains to?"

"That I am."

"And do you feel that you are worthy to shoulder this burden? Even should you come to the brink of death and face Old Man Darkness himself, would you hold true to your word?"

"I swear it, Your Radiance."

"Very well. I shall see to it that proper arrangements are made and that plans are drafted within the fortnight. You should get some rest, General, as it will be some time before your departure."

General Caerst bowed deep from where she knelt, raising both arms at an angle so the fingers crossed. The gesture resembled the wings of a falcon, signaling Alcaron's salute.

Without thinking, she was about to rise when, suddenly, *something* brushed along her side. The sensation was like that of a cold autumn wind, yet there was a hint of something more— something intelligent.

The experience made her freeze in place. She lifted her eyes, beholding the airy figures above the chamber. They danced in whimsical patterns around each other, circling the golden form that was Ilgrathié.

"You seem pale, General," She whispered. It was likely She also smiled. "My sylphs were merely observing you and your companion. Curious creatures, aren't they? So elegant, yet if you were to move one step against them you would be torn apart in seconds. I must admit, they make for wonderful bodyguards."

The halls reverberated with Her laughter, echoing a hundred times over in the minds of the Falconer and Aedas. Instinctively, she faced down as the astromancer remained unmoving. There came a sequence of footsteps before a soft hand caressed her chin. Caerst allowed her head to be raised up towards that scintillant face, and despite her efforts to remain calm and emotionless, tears flowed regardless.

"You have little idea how much faith I place in you." Her words were warm like sweet summer music. "Go forth and leave with my good blessing! I am expecting great things from you, General. Great things!"

Darkness dominated the room as the chamber door opened. A hooded figure passed through the silent shadows, the entryway clicking shut from behind. The silhouette moved to a nearby corner, producing a small tinderbox before lighting a few candles.

The low flames cast themselves over Aedas as he frowned. Outside, he could hear the celebration that was being thrown for the oncoming war. He imagined Mirungel would be enjoying several orgies tonight, as well as its assortment of potent narcotics. Such was the Ilgrathian way—nothing was ever achieved without indulging in the pleasures of the flesh.

Even now, he could hear the faint sounds of moaning in the distance, coupled with the odd scream of pleasure… or pain.

He hinged close his shutters, dampening the sound to an extent. He could tell that this night would be a most unholy one.

At least he was alone… save for his one and only friend. He looked towards the feline who slept in a corner. The tabby seemed to stretch herself momentarily before going inert once again. At either of her flanks stood tall shelves that were lined full of books and baubles, each organized in what seemed like an obsessive level of detail.

That was impressive in itself, as there were other containers filled with objects of all sorts: magic ingredients, tools of scrying, hourglasses, scrolls, books, et cetera. Alone they would have meant little to the average person, especially most Ilgrathians…

To the astromancer it was home.

Aedas pulled out the chair from under his desk, seating himself. He peered down and noticed that his hands were shaking.

Until now he hadn't realized how much of a toll his journey had taken on him. Of course, Harskul's shaman was partially to blame. Even after so many years, Aedas had recognized the man as his long lost brother. The feeling must have been likewise, for Gulizar had conveyed without words what the astromancer was thinking.

The old man wasn't the *actual* sorcerer after all—at least no more than any regular shaman. Instead, there had been another person who was the real magician…

Aedas sat there for a moment, closing his eyes while concentrating. The trembling subsided, his nerves relaxing somewhat.

A faint mewling then came to his ears. His eyes parted as he looked down to the feline rubbing itself against his leg. "Ah, Maelith! I'm glad to see you are doing well." He smiled. To most people it would have seemed strange that a cat should bear the name of one's past beloved. To Aedas, the tabby was a reminder of what he had once loved and lost.

His hand passed through the cat's supple mane. She reacted to the gesture with a purr, as he dropped a strip of jerky at her feet.

Once again he turned back to his desk before resuming his thoughts. How had it come to this, he wondered to himself. It seemed so long ago since he was allowed to live in peace with those he loved. Why couldn't the Ilgrathians leave him alone? Aedas had done so much for them. He couldn't go through all of that pain and suffering again—witnessing those he loved being burned and slaughtered for a cause under which they had no control.

But it arrived all the same. Only this time, *he* was the one who had wronged his people. Had he become so frail of spirit? So obedient to his masters' whims? Now there was nothing left of that little village—nothing left of the shaman he had once called his brother…

His hands resumed their trembling, yet he paid it little heed. He no longer cared for the memories of the distant past. There was only the thought of vengeance for what the Ilgrathians had done to him—vengeance against those who had caused his people so much agony.

His fist slammed against the desk. Below, Maelith regarded her master with a curious stare, utterly bewildered at what had upset him so. A moment passed before she lost interest, sauntering off towards another corner of the chamber, lost in the fancies which occupy the minds of so many cats.

Not a sound was made, as the man seemed like he was lost within his thoughts. That was when he moved to his feet, making his way to the door. Opening it, there was a little box which contained mail and the usual sort on its outfacing side. Only this time he sensed there was something else hidden inside.

The astromancer closed the door behind him, returning to where he sat and unfurling the vellum scroll. Yes, this was it—a register of all the slaves that had been taken from Harskul. He congratulated himself for his contacts and their resourcefulness. With any luck, they would hopefully not question why he wished for a copy.

He spared another look towards Maelith, feeding her a second piece of jerky. The tabby mewled happily in response, gorging on the treat as he redirected his attention towards the scroll.

The article held what seemed like two-hundred entries, but only a small portion of these were the slaves' actual names. His eyes pored voraciously over each moniker and description. A moment passed before he turned to one shelf, producing a nearby crystal ball used for scrying. Time would be of the essence, he thought, as it was possible that the sorcerer was still alive.

He hoped so. In the name of his brother, he would at least do that much.

III
Mines of Despair

Serithas and Zolan thrashed against their captors, struggling with the chains holding them in place. The Ilgrathians behind them smiled, as they saw Kolthan roaring out in fury, his one fist swinging among a half-dozen slavers.

The giant crushed the skull of the guard closest to him, crimson liquid spilling along his arms and fingers, the colors blending with the demonic airs of the gigantic cavern. It would be to no avail, they thought. The man was missing an arm, not to mention he was clearly exhausted by their hard journey from the south…

Still he would *not* give in.

"I will never relent in the face of evil!" he shouted in animalistic rage. "You will *never* get the best of me!!"

This provoked the two brothers, who continued their struggle with little regard for their lives. They begged to be reunited with their father, the greatest warrior Harskul had ever known. Their shouts echoed off the vast walls of that space, hot tears running down their cheeks.

Their resistance was short-lived, as the guards struck both of them in the head. Their vision went dark, and all they could do was give one final gasp before their remaining family was taken from them. Kolthan was left alive and thrashing before he was knocked out as well, dragged off into the depths of the darker tunnels…

Zolan awakened some time later, his head reeling from the blow he had taken. Looking to his side, he saw that Serithas was lying there. Groaning, he inched closer, jostling his brother awake with renewed desperation.

The sounds of agony were almost deafening. All around him came the shrieks and moans of the dying, and he could feel the stares of cannibals and rapists thrust in their direction, some closer than he would have liked.

He remembered the guards saying that such measures were needed to separate the weak from the strong, as only the latter could serve Ilgrathié.

The space in their prison-cell was small. It contained inmates just like themselves, though it was obvious the place was bustling, overpacked to the brim…

Zolan breathed in the rust-tainted air, mixed with blood, sweat, and feces, which nearly made him retch. He could see a ledge looming outside of their cell, giving a narrow passage for the guards and slaves they escorted.

He had never felt so alone, nor vulnerable, as he did now.

"Serithas," he whispered, his golden locks obscuring his eyes as he faced his brother. "Where is father? Don't tell me he is…"

The older boy moved up to his knees, his eyes burning with a lustful hatred. "Gone," was his reply. "Our father is likely dead for all we know."

The youth sat there, unbelieving, as Serithas violently struck his fist against the wall. He could not accept it. None of it made sense.

It had been several weeks since their village had been burned to the ground, seemingly for no other reason than to find a rogue magician. Everyone they had known was dead. They had been raped, tortured, and killed—all of them in this hellish place…

Time passed, and it became more than apparent that food was scarce. What little nourishment they received was thrown in like leftovers for swine in an overcrowded pen. The starving slaves fought over every scrap, clawing and scratching like beasts in order to stay alive.

Among that horrific scene of violence and depravity, Serithas and Zolan kept to themselves. The foodstuff was given out less and less, before it ceased entirely.

It wasn't long after that cannibals emerged as the dominant predator. Slaves were subjected to the ravenous appetites of men turned beasts, their hollow eyes hungering for flesh, bone, and sinew. Even the prisoners who starved were immediately devoured.

The brothers staved off these atrocious men for a time, their knuckles scabbed and bloodied from endless fights, as they chose to make do with starving instead. Still, the guards refrained from giving the captives their food. Their strength continued to wane, and before long pairs of malicious eyes began wandering in their direction.

Their first kill was one made together, as they were forced to fend off a savage who wished them harm… in more ways than one. They dispatched the man without injury to themselves, their fingers crushing into the man's neck until his breathing slowed and stopped. The other inhabitants took notice, and before long they were allowed to keep their corner, one that Kolthan had won for them previously.

Still, they wept and longed for death more feverishly than ever.

Their hands clawed along their stomachs, the hunger becoming more unbearable with each passing moment. They knew the end was drawing near, and then their souls would be in the hands of Old Man Darkness, that old master of death and the Great Beyond.

They had nearly given up hope when, suddenly, their cell-door was opened. Apparently, enough of their number had perished from hunger, and the slave population was back to reasonable levels. "Business as usual," said one guard to another, leading them out in turn.

Following their release, the brothers were given a small helping of food. They couldn't help but curse their fate, as higher brain function gave way to natural instinct. It was said by the guards that these small portions were needed. Slaves as malnourished as them ran the risk of having their stomachs burst if given too much.

Either way, they didn't care. To them the food was like ambrosia, and it was only a few moments before they were satisfied.

Soon afterward, they were forced along the precarious cliff-side. The ground beneath them widened as they stumbled forward, deeper into darkness.

They rounded a sharp corner and passed through an archway, a series of sanguine lights permeating the adjoining cavern. All around them slaves toiled without rest underneath a massive steel falcon. Gouts of white-hot fire shot from its nostrils, a walkway perched beneath its flaming beak. There the brothers could spot a shimmering metal passed from one worker to another—a substance they heard was called moonsteel.

Below this master forge were several dozen furnaces, each of them dug out in a cylindrical pit of its own. The fumes were piped in a series of tubes, snaking high up overhead, until they vanished through the cavernous ceiling. A lattice of catwalks spanned over each pit, with the occasional guard making his patrol, eyeing the slaves with a malicious grin.

The brothers steadied their trembling nerves, muttering a curse as they continued and were led into an adjacent cavern. Unlike before, the darkness here was absolute, save for the occasional guard who carried a lantern and whip at his side.

They stopped at a nearby wall, where they were given pickaxes and commanded to dig.

The work was hard and grueling, retrieving chunks of the silvery metal. Serithas had to fight from going to his rations as Zolan swayed in rhythm with his tool. Their hunger was fast returning, yet they would have to endure if they hoped to survive…

Several weeks passed as they were given a supply of food and water, oftentimes collapsing as they were brought back to their cells. Thankfully, these were not quite so crowded as they had once been. Even so, they had to fend off more cannibals, with some coming dangerously close to ending their lives. The guards never interfered during these times, as the cannibals themselves were accepted as a form of "population control."

Somehow they held themselves together, even when it seemed they had no desire left to live. There was some part of them that kept going, never giving into those who stood against them. In time they even felt a measure of their strength returning, *adapting* as their bodies became accustomed to their environment.

That was until one day, when they realized their food bags had been swiped. Serithas imagined that someone had taken it when their backs were turned. They would have to find it soon, as down here no one was far away from starving.

It seemed the guards were distant, as deduced by the glow of their lanterns. If the Ilgrathians saw them slacking in any measure, then that usually meant several lashes, if not worse.

They scoured the area. Perhaps with the time they had, they could find some trace of where their food had gone. Despite Serithas' argument to the contrary, Zolan insisted that they try not stealing from anyone else.

The boy eventually shrugged his shoulders, nodding as they investigated.

It wasn't long before they came across a slave who roused their suspicion. Despite the man's lean proportions, Serithas could tell that he was hiding something within his tunic, likely an inside pocket that had been stitched on.

The man was obviously a clever sort. And what was more, his bronze skin and aquiline features gave him away as Ilgrathian. An oddity, seeing as they were considered superior to all other races—even the wretches among their kind.

"You okay there, friend?" Serithas spoke with a grin, indicating the bulge along the man's shirt.

The Ilgrathian winced as he replied: "Doing just fine, thank you." He looked to where the boy pointed. "This is nothing," he remarked, "nor is it any of your business."

"Don't play coy with me," Serithas growled. "I know you've got food hidden in there, and I know that some of it's ours. I won't say it again: give us back what you stole!"

A moment passed yet there was no response.

"Please, just give it up," Zolan added, stepping closer himself. "We're only trying to make it by, just like everyone else."

"Then you best be moving on, friends. This food here is my property."

"Like devils it is!" Serithas gripped the man by his shirt, pulling him close. It was then that a long, thin dagger raised itself against the youth's neck. It pricked hard enough to bring a trickle of blood, hard enough to hurt…

"Like I said, you best be moving on. Lest you want a blade where it doesn't belong."

However, the man hadn't expected Serithas to react so quickly. He brought his knee up, slamming into the thief's groin area. Had this been a moment slower, then Serithas' neck would have been sliced nearly in half.

The Ilgrathian fell to the ground, reeling from the pain he had sustained. Serithas was quick to pin him there, retrieving the weapon before he could do aught else. The youth pocketed a few of the rations from his shirt, which proved to be at least half-a-dozen in total.

"All of these are yours?" he spoke in disbelief.

"Y-Yeah," the thief coughed, returning to his senses.

"Not anymore. These are mine now." He pocketed what rations he could while also keeping the dagger close. The Ilgrathian quickly changed his tune, however, as he was groveling on his knees.

"Please, have mercy! I confess that I stole it, but you've no idea what I went through to get those…"

The boy was about to turn away when he was stopped by Zolan. "We should leave him with a little," he said.

"Why? What has he done for us?"

"He's just trying to get by," Zolan explained, "and besides, he doesn't seem as dangerous as the others."

Serithas hesitated for a moment. He nodded, giving back a little more than a day's worth to the thief. Zolan added in a solemn tone: "And that's all we'll leave. If you try to attack or steal from us again, we won't be so merciful."

At that moment, there was a peculiar gleam which came from the boy's eyes. To anyone who gazed at him normally, they would have recognized it as the faint spark of lightning. But it was so pitifully weak—so inconspicuous—that only one who looked straight at him would have noticed it.

The Ilgrathian had done just that. His eyes widened, for he realized precisely what this was…

Magic.

"Just… who are you?" he inquired, looking at both of them.

Serithas studied his dagger, feeling a strange sort of connection with the blade. Of course, he didn't want to give away his real name, not in a place like this. And besides, he hardly even felt like the same person anymore.

"Steel," he muttered to himself. The name gave him a semblance of hope.

"Steel? An odd name if I say so myself. But if that's how you want to play it, then so be it." He chuckled. "Your mother must have loved you very much to call you that."

"She didn't. She's been dead for several years now."

"Now *that* explains a lot." He laughed even harder, tickled by his own twisted sense of humor. He turned to Zolan.

The younger boy pondered to himself. There was a strange satisfaction in choosing a new name, and it came quicker than he had realized.

"Stormbright," he said. "My name is Stormbright."

"Interesting." The Ilgrathian's eyes narrowed.

"Stormbright? What kind of a name is that?" asked Serithas.

The youth shrugged his shoulders. In truth, he wasn't sure why he had picked the name, other than being reminded of that storm from several months ago. His memory of it was still hazy, although he could recall streaks of lightning cascading through the heavens.

Some part of that resonated with him.

"It just… seemed right to me," he said bemusedly.

The Ilgrathian looked behind them. His eyes widened with realization. "Quick, the guards!" he exclaimed. "Both of you act natural."

Zolan and Serithas darted back to where they left their pickaxes. They had just resumed mining when the guards arrived. The slaver gave them a suspicious look, the light of his lantern blinding their vision, before they were again left in darkness.

A moment or two passed before the Ilgrathian joined them.

"Well, Steel and Stormbright, I think you two might be our ticket out of here. I can see that you've both got potential, and I could probably help with fending off some of these cannibals. Strength comes in numbers, as they say. In return, you could help me out when I decide to escape."

The brothers turned to each other, shrugging. Even if this thief was, in fact, lying to them, at worst that meant they would be tortured and flayed to death—a slightly more poignant alternative to their lives at present.

"What have we got to lose?" said Serithas. They smiled, turning to their companion. "Alright, you've got a deal."

"Excellent!" he said. "The name's Trilgar, and I can guarantee you've made the best decision of your lives."

Their correspondence with Trilgar remained pleasant, though the last two years were not without its own set of challenges.

It wasn't clear what the thief had in mind for their escape, though the man obviously had his connections. Through Trilgar, they learned of Alcaron's invasion against Divnarost, that strange nation lorded over by the gray-skinned Islirians, along with how costly the war was rumored to be. The Ilgrathians would need another victory or two before they could hope to see any reward…

That meant soldiers, not to mention moonsteel weapons and armor. Their labors were more difficult than usual, with the number of guards doubling from that of last year's, many showing scars or missing limbs due to the war effort. As a result, food was consumed in ever greater quantities. The slaves suffered all the more for it, with less and less being spared for themselves.

It would be over soon, they hoped. The brothers' plan, as Trilgar had told them, would have to be timed perfectly. It was just a matter of weeks before the armies and mercenary companies would be dispatched. Once that was done, many of the guards would refocus on other duties, then would come the time to make a deft escape.

They would have to make do for a little while longer. Steel and Stormbright had already learned much about themselves in the last several months. In many ways Trilgar had taken on Steel as an apprentice, with the youth trained in the various ways of the thief. Stormbright was taught with whatever weapons they could keep hidden, his skill with a blade growing by leaps and bounds.

In that time, Steel had grown in height as well as being a tad more muscular. Stormbright, on the other hand, remained small and wiry, although he developed an intelligence and cunning that were lost on the others. There were times when Trilgar would ask Stormbright about his affinity for magic. At this the youth would scoff. Him? A sorcerer? It was hard to picture it. And besides, the guards would take him away if they found out he *was* capable of such things.

It was during one day that the brothers and a third slave shoveled coal in a furnace. The kiln radiated with heat as the raw moonsteel was melted, purified in the blaze. The great falcon forge loomed over them, the avian creature appearing to smile, as their muscles ached and groaned.

A guard passed overhead along the catwalk. His boots rang with authority as his whip lay unfurled, trailing behind like a restless serpent.

The man halted. "You slacken in your work," he growled. His whip resounded in the air, lashing with a *crack!* Steel and Stormbright were eager to obey the Ilgrathian's command, as they didn't want their plans to fall apart now. Their breaths quickened as they kept pace the best they could.

"Faster!" The deafening sound came again, and the brothers felt their bodies being pushed to their very limits. They were covered in grime and soot, their nostrils inhaling the noxious coal dust, the furnace's heat blasting their skin, as it seemed like any moment that one of them would falter.

It was the slave nearest them who slipped and fell. The poor man wept and groveled as the guard descended to the pit's edge and cracked his whip, each lash met with a violent howl.

"Get up, you imbecile!" The slaver was clearly agitated, his frustrations from the war emerging in full force. Stormbright stepped in front of the whimpering soul, his look one of sheer defiance.

"We need a moment's rest. We'll resume as soon as he can stand."

The slaver scowled. "You forget your place, slave." This time the whip lashed against the youth, cutting along the brunt of his chest. The Ilgrathian gripped the edges of his tool, pulling it taught with one swift and terrifying motion.

Stormbright fell to his knees, choking and gasping for air; his whole chest burned like it was put over a fire. That didn't stop the whip from coming again and again.

"Bow down, you worthless whelp!" The boy didn't yield, and the guard's annoyance morphed into a seething rage. "You humans are so defiant and worthless. I will see you broken. I will see you begging for your deaths! *I will-*"

The slaver's words were cut short, as a lightning bolt seared through his chest. For a moment the man stood there, unmoving, looking down at the blackened scorch mark, before a blade followed the mysterious attack, slashing his throat.

Blood sprayed as the guard lurched forward, landing beside Stormbright and the slave he had protected.

With an effort he righted himself, seeing that Steel was standing along the edge. His brown hair barely masked his hatred as he spat on the corpse.

"He should have asked first," he said with a smirk.

Steel's expression softened as he focused on his brother. "Brother, what—what is wrong with your arms?!"

Stormbright looked at him in confusion… that is, until he looked down towards his outstretched limbs. Rivulets of lightning were traveling along them. Lightning! But he felt no pain.

"It can't be," he muttered to himself. After all the agony and torture they had endured, how could *he* have been the sorcerer the Ilgrathians were looking for?

His thoughts were cut short as a number of shouts erupted around them. Little did they realize that their murder of the guard was followed up by several others. The slaves' anger emerged like a raging torrent—a dam bursting from a single, vital crack—and it wasn't long before hundreds were crying out for liberation.

They were joined by Trilgar, as the two moved away from the pit's edge. "It looks like plans have changed," he said. "We move and escape through the nearby tunnels. Hopefully we can pass through the forbidden catacombs without being noticed."

"Wait, you didn't mention any catacombs from before."

"That wasn't part of the plan until now. Soon all of these tunnels will be swarming with guards, and that means strict patrol routes and surveillance for months, if not years. We've only one option—escape!"

Steel was about to interject further, but he could see the slaves around them were overpowering the guards, using their captors' weapons to their advantage. It was a full-on prison riot.

"I guess there's no better time than the present," he remarked, drawing his dagger as they followed the crowd. Trilgar unsheathed his own blade, and Stormbright found a sword among the slain.

Many Ilgrathians perished at the edge of their weapons as they pushed forward. They were joined by two others who fought in the chaos of the battle. No words were needed for them to know that they were all in this together, slaying, bleeding, and fighting alongside one another. The screams of their enemies resounded from hoarse throats, as their limbs were hacked away in a whirlwind of motion.

After several minutes of fighting, they broke away from the crowd. The tunnels were ahead.

The path twisted and wound its way onward as they lost sight of the guards. Thankfully, Trilgar seemed to know his way around well enough. They traveled for what seemed like hours in a foggy darkness, the walls of the area lined on all sides with a strange sort of ichor.

They emerged in a long carved out hallway. Just a short distance ahead they could spot a faint light which gave them hope, a sensation they hadn't felt for years…

"An exit," Stormbright breathed a sigh of relief. "I can smell fresh air coming from up ahead…"

The fog coalesced, gathering about them and obfuscating their path. The armed slaves moved forward regardless, yet it seemed that little progress was made.

They couldn't understand it. Their exit was gone; and what was worse, they could hear voices coming from their surroundings.

It was like all the denizens of the catacombs were resurrected at once. They could spot the semblance of faces, teeth, claws—all rising and moving in their direction. The ghostly things howled as their bony hands strove for the souls of the living, their glowing eyes longing for sustenance.

They slashed at the strange specters with their weapons; but it was to no avail. The spirits' bodies warped but they were unfazed. Before long only Steel and Stormbright remained conscious among their number. Their luck had run out in mere moments, and they were about to flee when they were grabbed up by their necks. They could feel the air sucked out of their lungs, their life essence drained by those horrific beings from the Great Beyond.

Steel cut wild and aimlessly, though it was little use. Stormbright tried channeling his newfound power, even though he hadn't a clue how to use it. It was his last hope in this desperate situation, yet it wasn't manifesting like he thought it would.

They were so close to freedom, so close to leaving behind their lives as slaves… But their time had come. Death was close, and soon they would join the specters in the afterlife.

"Enough!" a stern voice rang out.

The spirits relinquished their hold. The two brothers fell to the ground, coughing and sputtering, with little of their strength remaining. They spotted a figure emerging from the mist. His hands were outstretched in a gesture of benevolence, though the man himself looked like a withered corpse.

"A group of slaves has made it this far," he spoke in a stark baritone, his eyes staring into complete nothingness. "Little did you realize that I'm the master of these catacombs, and that only *I* can command these spirits with a trifle bit of concentration. Fools. You should have learned never to play tricks with the dead—nor a sciomancer, for that matter.

"I shall see to it that you are given punishment for your crimes. My superiors could always do with a bit more entertainment. As could I."

IV
Gladiators

When they next awoke, Steel and Stormbright found themselves in a prison-cell. Thankfully their hands weren't bound, though they were also alone.

Rising to their feet, the brothers looked out the bars of their cell door. An adjoining hallway loomed from whence they stood, cascading into formless nothing on either side.

Steel spotted a cell that was opposite from theirs. Though the area appeared empty at first, the clamoring of voices was recognizable to his ears. He realized that one of the voices was Trilgar—their fellow companion and cutthroat—along with the others who had helped them try and escape.

"Hey, Trilgar," he whispered, working carefully to project his voice across the corridor. "Looks like we're all in the same place, save for being in different cells."

"It certainly seems that way," replied the Ilgrathian. "All of us are doing fine over here. Things could have turned out worse, what with those spirits in the catacombs and that sciomancer skulking about."

"Just out of curiosity," spoke Stormbright, "what is a sciomancer?"

"They are conjurers of evil spirits," he said. "Though they're not quite as fearsome as necromancers or pyromancers, it would be foolish to mess with one in their territory."

"Oh."

A moment passed before Steel shouted in frustration. "Damn it all! We were so close to escaping! There's no way we could have known about that bastard living there…"

"Just let it go," said Trilgar, who was tossing pebbles in a corner. "We can't change the past now. We've got to keep moving forward, see if there's another chance for us to escape. The last thing we want now is to give up."

"I agree," interjected Stormbright. "At least we're safe for the moment."

"For the *moment*," echoed Steel with a hint of sarcasm.

"Trilgar," Stormbright continued, "do you have any idea of where we are? I can't say I've heard of a place like this, nor why it would be separate from the other cells."

The cutthroat moved his face closer to the bars before nodding. "Unfortunately, aye. I've heard rumors that there's a place where prisoners are taken—ones who live to become strong, that is— where either one of two things is done. First likelihood: our souls are extracted by Alcaron's magicians. I know little of what happens after that, only that I've heard the screams and I don't want to give it much further thought.

"The second," he continued, "is that they take us to the Gladiator Pit as entertainment. There we would be fighting for our lives against men and monsters alike."

"Wonderful!" shouted Steel. "Can there be any more tricks these Ilgrathians want to throw our way? Either way we're likely dead!"

"So it would seem," Trilgar nodded. "However, I suggest working out a plan, just in case there's a chance of us surviving."

Stormbright nodded, even as his brother kept pacing in circles. "I agree with that, Trilgar. What do you propose?"

"Simply that we stick close together as one, cover our flanks if we're surrounded. If needed I can try and pick these locks, see if I can scout out the place."

"If you try to escape," interposed a voice, "then you'll surely be caught. The guards are half-expecting you to do something like that."

"Who's that?" asked Trilgar, surveying the shadows from outside. They could see nothing. The voice echoed with startling clarity, as if the speaker were close by.

"I am a friend," it replied. "You should know that I plan on negotiating your release. For now, it seems you're set to fight here in the Gladiator Pit. I can only do so much until it is over, so be sure that you survive."

"No need to worry," said Steel, though he sounded wary regardless. "That said, what reason do we have to trust you?"

"You *don't* have one. Just know that I will be watching in the meantime. Security is most stringent within this part of the prison, and the guards are always on alert… As for your brother," he continued, "do *not* let them see what he can do."

The sound of footsteps echoed as the man departed. Steel couldn't place it exactly, but there was something familiar about that voice.

"It's strange," Stormbright murmured, facing his brother. "It's almost as if he knew about my…"

"Don't say it. For now let's just focus on getting out of here. I'm suspicious of all this myself, though it seems we've little choice. Wouldn't you agree, Trilgar?"

"Aye," the Ilgrathian nodded.

They continued planning for some time. After what seemed like an eternity of waiting, they heard the staccato of footsteps resounding along one end of the corridor.

They were Alcaronian guards with torches, dividing into two pairs as they addressed either group. "Stand back," commanded one guard, whose armor was made scintillant as it reflected his companion's torchlight. "Any false moves, and one of you loses a limb."

A key was produced. The door holding their companions was opened first, followed by their own. The two brothers were bound and led into darkness, following Trilgar and the others a short distance ahead.

The shadows grew fainter as they met a fork in the path. The right-facing corridor appeared to climb up in a sort of ramp, as their left continued at a flat angle. They were goaded right, forced along that steep umbral ascent. Eventually their path leveled out, with Stormbright (who stood in front) distinguishing a portcullis overhead.

A wave of glowing crimson light flooded their vision. They hardly noticed their shackles being removed, only a solid push forward was enough to remind them of their situation.

A loud creaking noise then shook their resolve. They realized that the portcullis was closing behind them. The gate sounded shut with a *clang*, their only method of escape cut off from them.

After a moment, their eyes adjusted to the unholy incandescence, as they found themselves within a large cavern. Their attention was drawn to the walls surrounding them, as they were lined to the brim with weapons suspended along a series of pitons. Above there came the chortlings of dozens of onlookers— merchants, gamblers, and hired swords—all of them packed over a number of rows.

Perhaps they were closer to the surface than they thought.

Steel and Stormbright steadied themselves as they moved to their feet. Off to their right they could see their companions. Trilgar stood nearest, who brandished a shortsword that was covered in rust and congealed blood. At either side were the other slaves they had known for such a short time; the first gripped a battleaxe of great proportion (as the man was burly himself) whilst the other held a shortbow, a quiver of arrows overhanging his shoulder.

Strangely enough, it was at this moment that Trilgar seemed most like a rodent. It was a queer thing to see an Ilgrathian who had been shunned by his people; but it was obvious the cutthroat enjoyed this.

"I always meant to ask, Trilgar," said Steel, as Stormbright searched for a weapon, "whatever brought you to these Slave Pits? Shouldn't you be living the high life up there with your fellow kind? I always thought you were hailed as some sort of superior race, yet you seem to hold little interest for it."

"A question I get too often," he replied, looking somewhat amused. "In truth, my brothers and sisters can keep their lofty ambitions to themselves. Here I feel more at home than I ever did up top. It was true that there were luxuries aplenty, and I can't say I didn't enjoy the wine and sex." His lips curled into a grin. "Still, there's no coming back after pilfering from your goddess' palace… the self-righteous slut."

"A fair point," the youth replied. It was then that Stormbright rejoined their number, brandishing a shortsword in his right hand while holding a wooden buckler in his left. A sling was holstered at his side with a bag of rusty pellets.

Steel followed suit, moving himself over to the arrayment of weapons. In the meantime the younger brother tested his blade. Though he found its edges were blunted by an amalgam of battles, the sword was surprisingly light and acquiescent to his movements. The buckler seemed natural for a boy his size, and it was a simple matter to drop it should he need to utilize his sling.

His brother returned with a long spear in hand. Although its edges were dulled, not to mention the wood being half-rotten in places, Steel smiled as he gave it a thrust. Apparently the young thief's movements hadn't slowed since their scuffle with the sciomancer. The weapon extended, before retreating with lightning-quick momentum. What's more, he had a shortbow wrapped over his shoulder… just in case.

"These should do well enough," he said. His brother's look, however, was one of doubt. Steel paid it little heed as he continued: "Even if the edges *are* blunted, a spear has enough impact on its own to kill someone."

Stormbright shrugged his shoulders, the five of them assuming proper formation. Along the front line there was Steel, Stormbright, and the burly ruffian holding a battleaxe. A short distance behind there was also Trilgar and the one archer.

The cheers from the onlookers became louder and more boisterous. It dawned on the gladiators that they were chanting in unison, though what they shouted was nigh impossible to make out.

"I hope they're cheering for us," muttered Steel.

"You might want to listen closer," replied the ruffian, who until this point had remained silent. "They're shouting a name I've never heard before: 'Brugmar,' they cry, 'King of Beasts.'"

At some distance across there stood another portcullis. It opened with a similar screech of agony, a number of nearby fissures belching forth clouds of volcanic fumes, obscuring what lay beyond. The earthy smoke billowed as if it led to some abominable hellscape. The gladiators steadied themselves for what manner of creature might come—be it man, beast, or aberration.

At first there was a low rumble before footsteps shook the ground underneath. The crowd halted their cheers, a deathly silence falling over the entire arena.

A savage roar echoed from the darkness. A pair of yellow-slitted eyes pierced outward like rays of sickly light. The beast lumbered into view, its mottled patches of fur hiding no shortage of scars among its bulk. To the gladiators, it seemed like it shared aspects of man and beast: it stood at three times the height of those who opposed it, its face showing as a strange mix between lion and wolf. Its mane was wild and unkempt, and in one hand was held a massive battleaxe.

The creature grinned, displaying several rows of jagged teeth. Not unlike a shark.

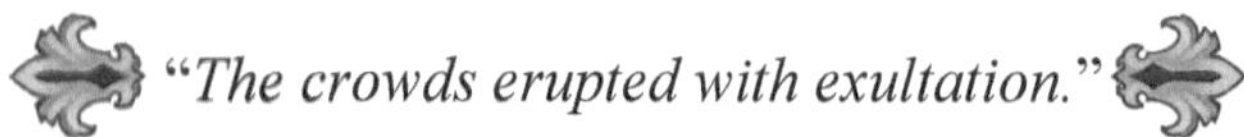

"The crowds erupted with exultation."

The crowds erupted with exultation. The Brugmar regarded its five opponents with ferocity, its savage eyes showing horrific strength.

Steel and Stormbright, Trilgar, and the other two slaves charged forward. They shouted in a wild, blind fury, though they were easily drowned out by the Brugmar and the crowd of spectators. Their opponent weathered their stabs and swings with ease, its iron-hard skin showing little sign of harm from their blades and arrows.

In turn it faced their one axe-bearing companion, picking him up with a furry paw as the others fought in vain. Its roar was deafening. For a moment the combatants stood there, disbelieving, as fangs pierced the man's torso, their friend torn apart by those gnashing, rending teeth.

The Brugmar gave out another howl, its maw stained by the blood and entrails of its victim.

Again the yellowish eyes swiveled, eyeing them with a malicious gleam. It took a frightening step forward; the survivors braced for the worst.

The fighting that followed was fierce, and the stench of blood permeated the air about them. The remaining slave loosed a volley of arrows, all while trying to keep his own fear in check. The thing growled as a number of feathered shafts bounced off its shoulder, with one going so far as to strike it squarely in the eye.

The beast swayed as it roared, for the moment being half-blinded. Steel raised his spear against the Brugmar. His hands shook terribly, as the fear of death was upon him. Regardless he charged forward, even scoring a vital hit along the creature's belly. The sheer force of impact did *that* much, at least.

Stormbright and Trilgar rejoined the fray as well. The former launched his sling pellets while the latter tried slashing at the beast's ankles. Though the Ilgrathian failed miserably in this respect, he nevertheless aided in flanking the beast.

The man-beast grinned wolfishly as it parried each attack with a swing of its axe. Many times Steel was forced to leap backwards, once by that humongous weapon, then again from a swipe of its claws. As this happened, Stormbright escaped a bite that would have surely beheaded him.

The Brugmar changed tactics, instead choosing to assail their one-and-only archer. The monster lumbered forward, its weapon rearing high overhead. The man let out a panicked screech before it landed with a crash. He wasn't quick enough to dodge, and so the two halves of his body split under a crimson mist.

The beast faced Trilgar and the two brothers, its remaining eye turning from a sickly yellow to a murderous red. Its gigantic bulk was covered in gashes, yet it showed no sign of slowing amidst its carnage.

"There must be some way we can kill this thing," breathed Stormbright. "Our weapons won't even wound it... Its skin is too tough..."

"You've got that right," Steel nodded in agreement. "I've slashed it along several places, though it's been for naught. I haven't tried cutting at its neckline, though. The creature guards itself right along that area."

"Then that's where we'll try focusing next." Stormbright turned to his companion. "Trilgar, can you circle around from behind and find a weak spot?"

The Ilgrathian nodded. "It shouldn't be a problem, considering our lives are on the line."

"Very good." They each steeled themselves, resuming their positions. "Let's hope we are prepared then…"

Just a short distance away, the Brugmar bellowed its war cry. Its clawed feet stomped and scratched along the ground in grating strokes; even the earth trembled at such a terrifying presence! It leaned forward, assuming a charging stance.

By the time it thundered to their position, the trio had divided and moved on either side. Steel and Stormbright kept the beast's attention whilst Trilgar slipped in between its legs, emerging out from behind as he leapt onto its back.

The thing didn't falter in the slightest. It raised its mighty fist, with Steel almost being pummeled once, twice, then thrice, as he maneuvered himself back-and-forth along the ground.

Suddenly, Stormbright was caught by a swipe of the Brugmar's axe. The sorcerer guarded with his buckler, though he was taken off his feet, as his only means of defense buckled under the impact. His arms flailed mid-air as he rolled some distance away.

"No! Zolan!" shouted Steel. At that moment he wished he could have tended to his brother, seen if Stormbright was alive or not. Yet he couldn't do so now, for the Brugmar would take advantage of that and they would both be dead.

He held his position, focusing his attention squarely on his enemy. He could see that Trilgar was hoisting himself atop the beast's shoulders. A dagger reared itself high over the Ilgrathian's head. It would have landed true, had the Brugmar not retaliated by thrashing about its arms and torso.

It didn't take long for the man's strength to fail, as he flew out a short ways from his former perch. He tried getting up, but the strain on his body was simply too much.

The beast didn't hesitate before taking the advantage. It brushed aside Steel's attacks, knocking him aside as it closed distance with the dazed Trilgar. The Brugmar raised its weapon, bringing it down with a thunderous crash!

Steel brought himself back to his feet, crying aloud at what remained of their friend. He swore terrible vengeance for what this monster had done, his anger burning deep inside of him. He hurled his spear in a rage, as well as nocking an arrow along his bow.

The Brugmar growled as the polearm plunged itself within its shoulder. It retrieved the spear with a snarl, snapping it in twain whilst it retaliated with its axe.

Stormbright found his footing as well, shaking off his bewilderment as there were two of them now. He and Steel exchanged a quick, knowing glance. Though not a single phrase was muttered between them, there came an improvised plan, one that both understood with perfect clarity.

Aiming his bow at the Brugmar, Steel released the arrow he had drawn. Several more came in rapid succession before their enemy charged again. Stormbright was quick to take advantage of this, drawing his sling and launching a pellet at the beast's snout.

Steel maneuvered around their opponent, seeing it was stunned and distracted, where he deftly retrieved Trilgar's shortsword. Though the blade was caked in his friend's blood, it remained unbent and perfectly usable.

He dashed forward, leaping and climbing just like Trilgar had done a few moments ago. The young thief held himself tightly along the back of mottled fur and muscle. It shook itself vigorously in an attempt to throw off its attacker.

Steel's grip didn't waver.

With a swift motion he rose to his feet, finding that he was standing on top of the creature's nape. He aimed his strike carefully, plunging the bloodied sword deep into the Brugmar's neck. His desire for revenge was all that mattered now. For a brief moment his rage overshadowed his remaining thoughts as he roared in anger, the rest of the arena going silent.

The man-beast howled its death throes, its body quaking under the violent strain of its wound. The youth lost his sense of balance, though he felt his enemy's movements growing weaker. It could have been a mixture of exhaustion, or perhaps some degree of blood loss, but he toppled forward as the creature collapsed in a lifeless heap.

He didn't move for several minutes. However, he detected a strange sound as he struggled to right himself.

Was that applause he heard?

Stormbright moved closer to his brother, pulling up the young man with a grimace. Steel looked about in a daze, seeing that the gamblers were cheering for the heroes who had conquered this "King of Beasts." It seemed strange that they should fight off one of Zirvonia's deadliest horrors, only to be met with a chorus of cheers.

Surely these Ilgrathians were the embodiment of wickedness.

He spared a brief glance towards Trilgar—or better yet, what was left of him. Though not a word was said among them, the brothers gave a respectful nod towards their friend, the only Ilgrathian who had helped them.

That was when Steel felt his brother's grip tightening along his arm. Stormbright cast him a knowing look, facing the onlookers above. "I think we've found our friend," he said.

The thief's eyes narrowed, coming across a figure among the shadows. Despite the man's subdued appearance, Steel recognized him as the hooded astromancer—the same person who had ruined their lives not two years ago.

"That bastard… How could he have known we were here?" he said, shaking his head in bewilderment.

"I think we've made ourselves a decent reputation since our escape," replied Stormbright. "My only question is *why* he's helping us."

V

A Voice in the Dark

"Enough, slaves!"

The cell door shut behind them, and Steel and Stormbright were left alone as the flaming lights disappeared, enshrouding them in darkness. Their fight with the Brugmar had been a harrowing one, not to mention the victory was left uncontested by the arena's spectators. Upon the brothers' egress, the Ilgrathians were left cheering, praising them as the humans who had bested the King of Beasts.

It made little difference now.

Time passed before they heard another stir of movement from outside. A sequence of footsteps reverberated from the nearby corridor, each stride echoing louder than the last. It was obvious who this man was. Steel's and Stormbright's stomachs twisted as they considered facing the astromancer—the same man who had instigated their shaman's death along with destroying their home village.

They spotted a shadow stretching against the far wall. The shape appeared vague and immaterial until it came into focus, taking on human proportions. The elderly man placed his torch in a nearby sconce. He took a slow step backward, the light of the brand illuminating half of his somber complexion, the other half remaining dim and obscure.

Steel regarded the magician with no small amount of disdain. At the same time, Stormbright looked with an equal measure of curiosity. The astromancer was exceedingly cold in demeanor, likely born from untold years of rule by his masters.

Yet there was something else hidden in those dark, unblinking eyes…

"It seems you've distinguished yourselves this day," he said. "And here I thought this little revolt you caused was just good fortune. I can see that there's more to you than at first glance."

"Spare us your pleasantries," said Steel. "If you think we can be swayed into doing your bidding, then you best be looking elsewhere. We are *not* your puppets!"

Aedas smirked as he replied: "I would have expected nothing less. If this meeting had been arranged under different circumstances, then I would have been forced to kill you for such a remark. Be thankful that is not the case." He took a step closer. "I'll be brief in what I have to offer you. You may do as you wish after that."

The thief went silent for a moment, sighing. "Make it quick," he said.

The astromancer nodded. "Do you happen to be aware of Alcaron's invasion to the south? That is, our war with Divnarost?"

The two brothers exchanged glances, a hint of confusion between them. "We both know of the rumors," said Stormbright. "At one point before the revolt, we were nearly worked to death because of it. I was flayed within an inch or so of my life, thanks to the guards."

"That was all for a reason." Aedas pursed his lips. "The invasion has been in effect for these last eighteen moons. And until the last three, everything was going exactly to plan. The Islirians fled before the might of our armies and war machines, their farms and villages razed like bonfires in the night.

"Yet when we found ourselves at the gates of Miracor, our fortunes changed for the worse. Their towers spewed cosmic fire which shattered our formations. And that's to say nothing of the specters who haunt the city walls—the very same star wraiths who could drain the life force of anyone close by. The city remains a final bastion for freedom, an anomaly in a world that's obsessed with order and discipline." He winced. "Need I insinuate who stands at the front lines?"

"General Caerst," said Stormbright, taking a wary step forward himself.

"The very same. Her efforts have been in vain thus far. The siege falters mid-course, and our armies are no match against our enemies' weapons. They are a wise and terrible people, these Islirians, ones who have persisted in spite of their curse. For any one of them who dies there is a star wraith emerging over their corpse. One-hundred years ago this nearly spelled out their doom, although now they have learned to live with it.

"I say this while offering to make you mercenaries. General Caerst has called for reinforcements, and several bands of hired soldiers have heeded her call."

"Mercenaries?" asked the thief, his voice rising. "Why would you expect us to fight for you? After all we've been through!"

The other shook his head as he kept his voice at a whisper. "You misunderstand. I am not asking you to fight for us, but rather that you should find some way to *join* the enemy. This won't be an easy task, and I would be remiss if I didn't mention the dangers involved. This is your best chance at living a free life—free from Alcaron."

"What is to prevent us from fleeing this mercenary group?" Stormbright asked.

"It is a possibility, though the likelihood of being caught is far greater. The Ilgrathians patrol the skies atop their rukh beasts—mighty birds who have a tendency for bloodshed. The alternative I present is the lesser of two evils. Even if you *were* taken prisoner by the Islirians, I think it's a better option than fleeing."

"But how can you expect us to trust you? How do we know that this isn't some farce, and you aren't misleading us?"

Steel was grinding his teeth. "Obviously, he can't be trusted. You destroyed our people. You destroyed our lives! Everything you do is a curse against humanity, you traitor! You coward!"

The astromancer bowed his head. "You are right," he said. "It is through no one else's fault but my own that you've suffered the way you have.

"But you should know that the Fields of Man were once *my* home as well. Gulizar was *my* brother, and together we had a life of peace, free from the Ilgrathians!" He stopped, taking a deep breath. "That was long ago. There was little I could do to prevent your shaman's death after he had volunteered himself for it. Even then he was the same man I had always known and respected. Now he's gone…"

He sighed. "I like to think there was a reason for his sacrifice. I know he died protecting both of you. As best he could anyway." He pointed to the younger of the two brothers. "Especially you."

"What?" said Stormbright, bewildered.

"You are a sorcerer. Likely a powerful one too if my *inner sense* is anything to go by. You should consider yourselves lucky that no more than a few guards noticed your little episode. I know this through a connection of mine; the rest have since been bribed so the information remains a secret. You don't know how bad the alternative could have been. If the jailers had found out about your *gift*, then you would've been taken to the Soul Cistern, tortured until your mind and body relinquished its grasp on your soul."

"Just like father…" Stormbright spoke to himself.

"Not so. I have come to tell you that your father is alive. Of that I made sure through my connection. The effects of the Soul Cistern have weakened him somewhat, though he is at least cognizant of his surroundings."

"You lie," Steel growled.

He shook his head. "I've locked him away in a separate cell, though this might change should more souls be required. He has instructed me to relay you a message: 'Hold fast to your training and never relent—not ever in the face of evil.'"

Steel stopped himself from going any farther. He swallowed dryly as he slumped along the cold floor. "That sounds like father, alright," he said.

Stormbright nodded in agreement, wiping away his tears along his sleeve.

Aedas continued: "I'll do my best to see he isn't killed. Even so, it's imperative that you take your leave. The road ahead will *not* be an easy one. But if you can best a Brugmar in battle, then that raises my hopes somewhat."

A silent moment passed before Stormbright looked towards his sibling. "So what is our plan, brother?"

"The plan," interrupted Aedas, "is that you will be led topside and recruited by a mercenary company. Do not fret, for I have already pulled a few strings myself. Commander Talik from the Black Tortoise Company should be willing to take you on. He is a most generous and amiable man, and I couldn't think of anyone better to help you. I cannot join myself, for I require time to free your father. He is weak and unfit to fight; thus I'll have to find some other means of releasing him, possibly by faking his death."

"Very well, then." Stormbright relaxed just a trifle, a real sense of elation overcoming him. It felt so strange to smile after what they had been through, but now was as good a time as any.

The astromancer's expression didn't budge. "There's one last detail you should be aware of," he said. "General Caerst has recruited a new lieutenant. This Ilgrathian is a magician not unlike myself, though there is something different about him. Many of us refer to him as a sciomancer, or one who communicates with dead spirits."

"Does the man resemble a corpse?" queried Stormbright.

Aedas winced. "I'm assuming you've had dealings with the man in the past?"

"Yeah. Something like that," Steel replied. He turned to his sibling. "I don't know about you, but I think it's about time we gave our enemies some payback. What do you say, brother?"

Stormbright smiled. "Agreed," he said.

VI
Thrust on the Front Line

"I'm assuming all the preparations have been made?"

"Exactly as you commanded, General." The sciomancer regarded her with an aloof stare.

"Very good," she said. "Are you sure that your summoning will succeed? This is not some trifling invocation, Dimorn. The loss of life could be immense should you fail…"

"Do not worry, General. I have communed much with the spirits over these last several nights. The creatures of the Great Beyond hunger for the flesh of our enemies, as has been their wont since time immemorial."

"I do not doubt their ferocity," replied General Caerst. "It is their loyalty which I find concerning. I know of many sciomancers who can wrest control from entire legions of spirits. However, I've also heard the stories of when they lose control. Can't we find some means of controlling the star wraiths? Surely that would strike greater fear into our enemies. Our victory would be assured then."

The sciomancer shook his head. "I have already tested that. Alas, it has given me naught. I'm not certain as to why the star wraiths cannot be controlled…"

The Falconer frowned, disappointed that she couldn't use the Islirians' age-old enemies against them. Instead, she would have to trust the sciomancer's word on the matter; invoke the creatures who dwelled in the myriad other realms that made up their existence. Still, something deep down told her that the risks would be great…

She pushed away the thought, reminding herself that the chance for failure was always something to be considered.

"Then you are confident with this army of ghosts?" she continued.

"Not ghosts," interrupted the sciomancer. "Demons. And yes, they will heed my call so long as their hunger drives them."

"*Demons?*" she growled. "How could we accept the aid of such creatures? This is a crusade, Dimorn! Not some bloody ritual made for heathen sorcerers."

"You forget that this is why you came to me in the first place. The Islirians are more cunning than you initially thought, and so other means must be considered. The star wraiths cannot be killed by normal means; only magic can do the trick. Summoning the demons will tie them to my sciomancy, thus making them vulnerable. That should prove effective against repelling the star wraiths."

The sciomancer cocked his head. "You're also the one who requested me personally, knowing of my capabilities as well as the risks involved."

A moment passed before she nodded, sighing reluctantly.

"Then you are aware of my methods, as well as what it means to recruit a sciomancer?"

General Caerst nodded again. "I am. In that case, you may do what you will. But promise me that Miracor shall be conquered after this. In truth, I can scarcely tolerate more of this blasted waiting! Ilgrathié expects results from me, and I mean not to fail Her."

Dimorn nodded. "I wouldn't have expected anything less."

A short time elapsed before the brothers were hailed by the guards. The pair of armored figures stood stolidly before them as they unlocked the door to their cell, their faces bearing more than a hint of frustration.

"You should consider yourselves lucky," announced one Ilgrathian, regarding them with a scowl. "It's not every day that prisoners like yourselves become mercenaries. If I had a say in the matter, you would be left rotting here for the rest of your pathetic lives. That Brugmar was our pride and joy—a real crowd pleaser. But it seems that Fate can be a cruel mistress…"

Manacles shut themselves over the brothers' wrists. The shadowy corridor loomed out before them in a vast stretch of infinity. Neither of the two could distinguish more than a few cubits ahead of them, though the guards moved towards the unknown as if they had done so a thousand times previously.

They plodded onward for what seemed ages before coming to a ramp. It rose at a steep angle, coiling around itself. Eventually they found a bright light coming from overhead as they ascended as one group. The glare nearly blinded them in its potency.

The path leveled out from underneath as they passed through a large doorway. The brothers sensed a familiar warmth on their skin; they realized it was the sun looming above them.

Stormbright looked to his side, seeing that Steel was experiencing the same emotions he was. He smiled. It seemed that more had happened within these last few days than their whole two years as slaves. The thought gave him a strange sort of elation, one he was exceedingly thankful for.

Even Steel couldn't help but ease up a trifle. His hatred diminished as the bright sounds of the city bustled around them, the warmth of their surroundings filling him with a newfound zest for life.

They continued along the crowded streets, which were filled with the delicate bronze faces of the common Ilgrathian. The city-goers scowled as brothers and captors walked past, being led through the high rising city walls. The belts of gardens and orchards beamed as they ringed about Mirungel. The party ventured a short way before they faced a hillside pavilion.

They recognized the stone cottage, as it was rather small and quaint when compared to the nearby capital that dwarfed it in size. There was also a large cluster of tents that surrounded it. Their colors ranged from many various hues: shades of emblazoned jet, violet, blood crimson, and turquoise. Each soldier wore a unique raiment that was in accordance with his company, and Steel and Stormbright noticed that these men were even throwing the odd playful insult at one another. All in good fun, it seemed.

Soon thereafter they were led inside the pavilion. It was a small and comfortable living area. Many armored feet plodded along the low-ceilinged halls about them, as they were introduced to the human who called himself Commander Talik. The mercenary leader proved to be surprisingly amiable, much like the astromancer had described, though his words were tinged with a flare of military discipline. The guards released the brothers from their chains, leaving many of the Ilgrathians present with a feeling of disappointment.

Steel and Stormbright were then briefed on the nature of their task, which included the long journey south along with orders for when they would arrive outside Miracor.

The commander smiled as he concluded: "I should have you know that my orders are simple—so simple, in fact, that even a blasted fool could understand it. Should I tell you to advance, then you will do so. Should I tell you to retreat, then you will do that as well. Do I make myself clear?"

"Aye, sir!" they replied. The two were quickly dismissed, and for the first time in ages they felt a marginal degree of cheer. The fiery glow of the sun settled a stone's throw over the horizon, and the moons Taldriath and Bruann could be spotted among the gloom.

That night as they pitched camp, the brothers partook in an assortment of strong drinks and viands, including a delectable hog set over a fire. Steel found welcome company among their fellow humans, and Stormbright discovered that the few Ilgrathians among them were also kind. So great was the difference between their lives as slaves and mercenaries that they nearly choked up in tears. They had survived so much…

The sun rose once again, the various mercenary companies wandering frantically about the camp. Bundles of canvas were folded as fires were doused in a matter of minutes. Apparently the brothers hadn't joined a moment too soon, for they were roused from slumber as their brothers-in-arms began the southward journey in earnest.

Their march was a steady one, and the column spanned not more than five pairs of feet across. The twain marched as one with the Black Tortoise Company, their garments a similar jet black hue. Each wore a shirt of mail that was reinforced by a black cuirass, greaves, and helmet. Neither of them felt that their armor was comfortable, as it hindered mobility and one's own sense of balance. Regardless, they shouldered their packs and strode onward. And though their journey was an exhausting one, Stormbright found his spirits rising as the distance grew between them and Alcaron. It was so strange to feel the sun heating their backs—to hear the birds, wind, and trees singing their melodies when compared to the hell they had endured.

Stormbright breathed deeply, savoring the sweet smells of the outside world, those hyacinths, lavenders, and rhododendrons.

Steel chuckled upon noticing this from his brother. Even he couldn't help but do the same.

Some time passed before they detected a sharp beating sound from overhead. The sorcerer gazed up as Steel fingered the dagger at his side. The forms moving above them bore a likeness to falcons, at least judging by their long wing-span and the shape of their tails. Only these creatures were more powerful as they were slightly larger than horses, their wings stretching more than ten-cubits across as they emitted a harrowing, blood-curdling shriek.

"It seems the Almari have decided to join us," mused one mercenary, standing beside Stormbright.

"I know a little about them, myself," he said, "but what are these 'Almari,' exactly?"

"They're Ilgrathians who ride atop rukhs," the mercenary replied. "Don't kid yourself, for they're the most vicious soldiers when riding into battle. I've seen many good men with their entrails left askew from those razor-sharp talons, or ones who've had their eyes plucked out by the rukh's beaks. They are a terrible combination, my lad, and I would caution against getting too close to one."

Stormbright looked up to the dozens of silhouettes circling over them, shuddering. If he and Steel ever hoped to return and rescue their father, then he prayed they wouldn't encounter such malignant creatures.

So continued their journey as the road ahead grew wild and more dangerous. Lone crags jutted out on either side, all while the fields around them transmogrified into an array of rocky cliffs and ledges.

The going was rough, and they were left exhausted at the end of each march. However, the brothers had never felt more alive, as they were given sufficient food and drink—the likes of which they had nearly forgotten since their time as slaves.

"This damn fog!" Steel swore in a bout of frustration. The youth swiped vigorously at the thick veil surrounding their company. It yielded little to his efforts, as they were forced to move through a blinding shroud of mist. "I can barely see beyond my hand! How are we supposed to fight if we can't spot our enemies?"

The other mercenaries seemed to share the sentiment, although they didn't speak for the majority of the trip. The mist curled about their armored boots like the hands of some horrific phantasm. A gust of chilly air came along with it, one that froze the bones of those present.

The hairs raised on the back of Stormbright's neck, as he pondered if the fog was anything more than a natural occurrence.

At last they came into a wide vale where the mist wasn't so dense. Though the air was clear for the moment, their senses of hearing and smell were in a heightened state, as the chill and paranoia remained the dominant stimuli among them. They saw the war camp was close at their side. The sounds of other soldiers could also be heard a short distance away.

The rest of the valley was bereft of life. It was as if the humans and Ilgrathians had been isolated, lost in a land which somehow beckoned them into the murky plains beyond.

While entering the encampment, Stormbright stole a quick glance southward. A series of ghostly lights winked out at him from the fog, which, judging by the soldiers' indifferent expressions, only he seemed to notice. He was reminded of Aedas' words, specifically how the star wraiths moved along the city's perimeter.

The two were goaded into the center of the outpost, all while their fellow soldiers grouped around them. A horn sounded nearby; the commanders and captains—both Ilgrathian and human— gathered under the folds of a central pavilion. Among them all was *her*, the very same woman who had ruined their lives two years ago…

General Caerst.

The silence was palpable as those of the Black Tortoise Company, along with the remaining mercenary groups, stood in rigid rank-and-file. Steel and Stormbright were flanked on either side by dozens of soldiers. With any luck, Steel surmised, that *whore* wouldn't notice them…

The order to disperse hadn't been given yet. They stood in silence, a peculiar dread hanging in the air.

"Hearken, one and all!" she announced, addressing the war camp in its entirety. "Today we steel ourselves for war, for the final assault of Miracor is upon us. I have already briefed your commanders on our situation. Your role will be of no small importance as you serve us along the frontlines. We of Alcaron shall join you shortly. For now, know that your pay shall be more than adequate, and that your contributions to this war will be regaled by minstrels and poets the world over."

Marching orders were given soon thereafter, and the brothers were forced away from their sworn enemy. It seemed she hadn't noticed them. They departed camp along with the others, trudging along damp grounds which became soggier with each step. It didn't take long for them to arrive outside the city. Following a steep escarpment, the landscape dropped considerably before expanding in a vast empty stretch, completely barren other than the odd ruined house speckled here or there. Miracor hugged the side of a mighty river bank, with its walls spanning over fifty cubits in height, though this did little to stop the mercenaries from surrounding it.

The strange lights intensified as the brothers crested a hill, the armies and siege engines moving slowly beside them. The front gate was very close now, and their skin crawled from what they saw ahead.

Stormbright swallowed as he spoke. "Are those…"

"Star wraiths," Steel replied.

It was a peculiar sight to behold, for Stormbright had always pictured the star wraiths as resembling their former living selves. Only less corporeal. Instead these were beings more abstract, more *strange*, altogether. The specters shimmered as their bodies were like tears in the fabric of reality, all showing the same veil of stars and cosmic gasses. The celestial backdrop remained in place, as the ethereal bodies flitted like wisps of smoke, the two elements acting independent of one another.

The overall effect was most disorienting. The brothers would have doubted that these were even sentient creatures until they saw the white slits of eyes looking in their direction, each pair attached to a shroud that parted and reformed like some piece of a greater puzzle.

Above the drifting figures came those azure lights which were the Islirian towers. A large crystal—undoubtedly of strange and arcane design—perched atop the spindly bulk of each.

The walls themselves showed no signs of movement. To the ignorant outsider, it would have seemed the entire city was abandoned some time ago, naught left but a ruin that had been overtaken by lichen and horrific specters.

Steel knew better; his senses told him as much.

"We're being watched," he said.

Stormbright nodded. "If we can't cross in time, then it might be worth us fleeing. Even if we were intercepted by the Almari, we could always take our lives as a last resort." He looked up to his brother, the reality of his words sinking in.

"It won't come to that," Steel replied. "We will just have to survive."

"And what about my… gift?" The sorcerer held out his hands, implying the magic he had used as part of their escape. "I'm not even sure if I can use it again. I just don't know how…"

"Stick close to me. And keep your sword about you."

Reluctantly, Stormbright nodded. Looking onward, he could see that the specters were gathering into one gigantic, undulating mass. Malicious eyes peered onward to where the brothers stood, their bodies quivering with a ravenous appetite for the living.

It was then that Commander Talik shouted from behind, his voice sounding like death itself. "Charge, men! For the glory of Alcaron and your own sakes! Charge!"

So the Black Tortoise Company charged forward, attacking while several units ran at their left and right flanks. The star wraiths' retaliation was immediate as the two forces collided. Swords and polearms were driven into the sickly phantasms. Shouts and screams and curses all became intermingled with the chaos of battle brought to a roaring crescendo.

The mercenaries' skill was futile. The star wraiths would disperse, reform some distance away, before resuming their attack. The bodies of their victims became shriveled husks as their essence was drained in an instant, their remains little more than mummified corpses.

It was then that the Islirian towers shimmered with vibrant and terrible energy. This was followed by sapphire rays piercing the grounds below. The beams criss-crossed as they decimated the invading armies, setting fire to the damaged machines of war. Human mercenaries shrieked while their flesh burned. Limbs were severed and immediately cauterized, so great was the effect of that magic!

Seeing all of this happening, Steel and Stormbright surrendered all hope of their plan succeeding. The upper portion of a ballista collapsed at their right flank. They had barely dodged the wreckage of it. Now was a desperate battle for survival above all else, and there could be no way out save for escape.

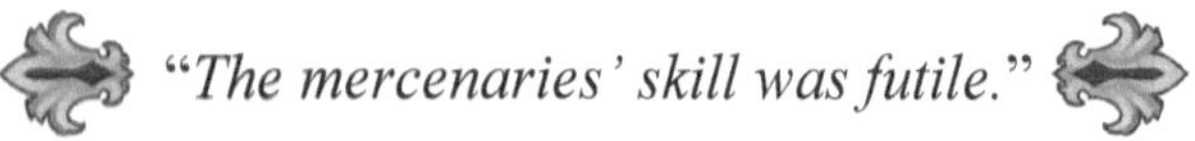

"The mercenaries' skill was futile."

They broke away from their enemies. Their efforts were for little gain, however, as the beams would stray a mere arm's span away from them. Each time they would be forced to hide and seek for cover. Progress was made between the two of them, though their speed wasn't much faster than a snail's.

Moving through the ruins of a nearby farmhouse, Stormbright redirected his gaze towards the distant rampart above. It was obvious that a number of figures were running along its top edge, hurling boulders onto the tiny invaders below. He did not doubt that these were the Islirians Aedas had spoken of. What shocked him more so was how composed they seemed while facing up against a larger enemy.

A peculiar screeching sound met his ears. Looking up, he and Steel could see that a flock of Almari were soaring over their heads. The Alcaronians held themselves closely to the lean bodies of their mounts as they careened over the walls, circling about the structures that spewed fire and death.

Javelins and lances were hurled against the crystalline spheres. It wasn't long before the beams shifted focus, and the Almari were caught amidst a ceaseless barrage of magic fire. The surviving rukh riders were forced to make a harried retreat. And though the Almari's attacks were ferocious, only a few of the spires showed any signs of damage. Not one of them faltered as they continued releasing fiery oblivion on their enemies, a feat made possible by the most primal of sorceries.

Stormbright crouched in bewilderment; he didn't so much feel like a soldier as he did a swine awaiting its slaughter.

A hand gripped his shoulder. "It's time for us to leave," shouted Steel. "The magic towers are directed against the Almari. Quickly now!"

The youth didn't respond as he sensed something strange. It was the scent of magic. How he knew so was uncertain to him, but it registered all the same.

He looked behind, his eyes resting on a figure who stood atop a distant crag. The Ilgrathian's arms were outstretched, and Stormbright could hear the faint murmurings of eldritch signs carried along the winds.

"It's the sciomancer," he murmured, losing all sense of hope.

That was when the air shifted about them. The very fabric of reality appeared to distort as if it were being condensed—compressed—into hundreds of solid forms. The shapes expanded, materializing into flesh. Black, scaly wings outstretched themselves as the bird-demons came howling forth into existence, claws and teeth bared for all to see.

The two brothers stood aghast as the creatures soared towards Miracor. Stormbright could see the Islirians turning away in fright whilst their enemies flapped overhead. He could sense their thirst for blood—the hunger driving them relentlessly forward.

The sensation was powerful. Too powerful, in fact…

Something was wrong. He noticed that a few of the fiends had remained near them, much to their dismay. It wasn't long after that the demons made their advance. The slaughter began in earnest, as humans and Islirians were rent asunder by those slavering jaws, shearing claws, and crooked beaks. Only a few moments had passed before hundreds of soldiers perished on both sides—a bloodbath that would have shamed even the proudest of military commanders.

The sciomancer stood there, shocked, as he witnessed the tenacity of the things he had summoned. The hellspawn howled with frightful abandon as they tore their way through *both* armies, their scaly hides bathed in the blood of their prey. The creatures slew without discrimination or mercy. The realization had dawned on him that more mercenaries were being killed than their actual enemies.

"Dimorn! You weak, insolent fool!" the Falconer roared. She darted forward like a mad demon herself, furiously striking him with the back of her hand. The force was sufficient to bring him to his knees, nearly enough to break his jaw.

He had never known a woman to be so strong. But then again, General Caerst was no ordinary woman.

"You have sabotaged this invasion, and quite possibly forfeited both our lives!"

"But General, I could not have foreseen that my demons would wrest control-"

"That is enough!" She struck him again, this time bringing tears to his eyes. The Ilgrathian recoiled in shame, humbled by the weight of his actions. Eventually, she regained her composure. "I must sound the alarm; signal our retreat. Should our lives be spared, know that it will be *you* who atones for this misdeed. Is that clear?"

The sciomancer nodded as he salvaged his pride. "Aye, General," he said. "It will be as you command."

The two brothers backed up as their enemies pressed forward. Several of the creatures lay at their feet, slashed and mangled from the use of their weapons. It was not enough. They were fast reaching their breaking point.

Steel and Stormbright were covered in wounds. In fact, it was only through sheer force of will that they remained standing.

"There's so many of them…" Stormbright looked around, seeing that they were the only ones left standing under a sea of demonic bodies.

"Don't give up now! Just keep pushing forward, no matter the cost!"

"But I-I…"

A dozen more of the hellish creatures came towards them. The two weaved and dodged as best they could, sustaining the most superficial of wounds in the process. That is, until one sank its teeth into the thief's shoulder, pinning him helpless to the ground.

"Brother!" Stormbright shouted as he thrust his blade into the monster's temple, killing it instantly. The jaws retracted, enough for Steel to push it off him. "You can't die like this, Serithas. We've got to keep moving, just like you said."

"R-Right." Steel moved himself to an upright position. "Zolan, behind you!!"

The youth turned in the nick of time. Just so that he noticed his hands were radiating with electricity. It coursed along his arms, cascading down his fingertips. The demon could do little in retaliation before it was engulfed by the explosive energy, turning into a charred husk after a few seconds.

"What! But… But how?!"

"Don't question it," Steel responded, his desperation overriding his curiosity. "Just focus while you can." A half-dozen more came against them, but they were driven back by the thief and his spear. Alas, the haft of it snapped as another fiend clawed at him from the side. The weapon was effective in preventing them from coming closer. But it was gone now…

That left only his dagger.

Stormbright brought up his hands again, scorching the demons who remained with a shockwave of lightning.

Their enemies didn't relent as the two were surrounded. The fiendish things howled and shrieked against those who dared stand against them. Steel and Stormbright pressed their backs against one another, the former holding his dagger as the latter discarded his broken blade, stretching lightning between his fingertips.

It was all or nothing. Do or die.

"Do you think we can take them?" muttered Stormbright.

"Of course," Steel laughed in response. "Are you scared or something?"

"No," the boy smirked, feeling the true extent of his powers driving him forward, imbuing him with newfound confidence. "I think we can do this."

What followed thereafter was witnessed by few—either the brave spectators who watched along Miracor's walls, or the remaining Ilgrathians who fled. Even Steel and Stormbright would remember little of it themselves, so furious were their actions in the midst of battle. The soldiers who gazed on from afar would espy the blur of a dagger slashing fore and aft, coupled with lightning eviscerating everything in sight. The two who stood in that chaos moved together as one, their senses heightened to their peak as they danced in perfect unison, magic and blade complementing one another, as if it were always meant to be.

They fought for hours without ceasing. Soon, the battlefield was laid barren of all life, and for miles about there lay heaps of dead humans and hellspawn and broken war machines. Even the star wraiths had fled among the chaos, for they had sensed a threat to their survival. Whether that was Steel and Stormbright, or the demons who fought against them, no one could say.

At last, it was the two of them who were left standing. The brothers looked about themselves as they staggered, slumping to the ground under a wave of paralyzing exhaustion.

All went silent and still. That is, except for the few who removed themselves from the wall, emerging onto the vast plain below…

VII
Beyond the Border

A thin stream of light filtered through the dusty chamber. Stormbright awoke in its shadow, his arms and legs both bound.

"Oh, Serithas," he whispered. His brother lay next to him. Though it appeared the thief's wounds had been bandaged, he didn't move at all. The youth tried slipping out a hand from his bonds; the cord which held him was well-knotted, and so it was difficult to move himself over, even just a little.

There came the sounds of muffled footsteps, as they passed through a large, wooden door. The boy stiffened as the noise became louder, the portal opening wide as it scraped on rotting hinges. A thick moldy smell permeated the room, the humidity causing Stormbright's clothes to cling to his back.

"It's time to wake! Both of you!" announced a man with a strange accent. He took a confident step forward, along with a half-dozen others who followed next to him. "You have been accused of war crimes against Divnarost. For prisoners of war, there is no trial among the common people." He smirked. "You are in my hands now. My word is law. I am judge, jury, and executioner."

Stormbright spared a glance towards his captors. All but one of them was clearly male, their skin being a gray ashen hue. Their garb consisted of leather tunics and sack-cloth pantaloons. Orbs of jade, ivory, and azure stared at the brothers with considerable reproach, as they foretold of lives consisting of endless, unremitting savagery.

The leader stepped closer to the twain. His lean muscles tensed along his wiry build, his scowl showing itself more as he continued: "Tell me, prisoner, were you the one who summoned the flying demons—the ones who attacked us along the wall? I must admit, you had given a most dazzling display of lights before you fainted."

The sorcerer shifted onto his side, facing the gray warrior directly. "No, that summoning wasn't my doing. I know of the man who conjured the demons though. His name is Dimorn, though we refer to him as 'the sciomancer.'"

He saw the Islirian step aside, allowing the lone female of their group to move forward. It was almost frightening to behold the elderly woman's wrinkled, hag-like appearance—a direct contrast to the muscle-bound men who surrounded her. There was a flash of wisdom in her eyes as she regarded him. Her lips split into a warm smile, a single hand outstretching itself towards Stormbright.

"Do not worry yourself, Ya'utet," she murmured in a smooth voice. "I can tell the boy speaks the truth."

The warrior nodded, kneeling casually on one knee. His eyes glared into Stormbright's own. There was great pain there, and Stormbright felt vaguely disturbed by it. "Tell me," he said, "if you are not the one who summoned these creatures, what was this magic you invoked? The both of you were surrounded by it when the demons fled and the Ilgrathians were routed."

The boy nodded his head. "It is lightning," he said, "though how I received it I'm not sure."

He grimaced, perplexed as to how something so destructive could have been caused by his own hands. "Before this, my brother and I were enlisted as mercenaries. We were told by an astromancer that I was a sorcerer, though at the time we kept it a secret. We were prisoners. If my abilities were found out, then it would have meant death for both of us."

"But how did you know that this astromancer would help you?" spoke Ya'utet. "We have spoken with many humans in the past, and they have told us much concerning the Ilgrathians' ferocity."

"That's because he was also human," replied Stormbright. "Thanks to Aedas, we were enlisted as mercenaries and sent here to fight… even though we didn't really have a choice. If it wasn't for his help, then we would still be slaves to the Ilgrathians."

The Islirian faced the woman to his side. "And what do you think of this, Shariz'lan?"

Her words came like a whisper. "I believe there is much more to these two than it seems," she said. "Both hold a great talent and greater pain still. Especially this one…" She pointed towards Stormbright.

"Then do what you must," said Ya'utet, standing and taking a few steps back.

Stormbright felt a pair of bony fingers resting along his forehead. "Calm your mind," she said soothingly. "Now, try to remember what happened before."

Reluctantly he did so, and his mind wandered beyond fathomless voids of time and space. There came a great stirring as the chamber shifted in mood. The crone tore herself away, as lightning curled about his arms and hands.

The surrounding warriors gave out a cry, leveling their spears in defense. Shariz'lan rose to her feet, holding out her hands in a halting gesture.

"I am fine!" she shouted. "This is only natural for a sorcerer who can't control his powers."

"But the man could be a danger to us all," expostulated Ya'utet. "Who knows what destruction he might cause?"

The crone inched closer to the youth. The Islirian warriors saw that the lightning which engulfed the boy was now dissipating.

In his mind, it was like a dam had been broken, a torrent of forgotten memories crashing through. He remembered the lightning and thunder of the storm from two years ago, along with the loss of control he felt as a voice called out to him. He recalled his sighting of Calamtu—that towering god-figure made up of clouds and energy—as well as how something had awakened deep inside of him.

"Stormbright," he muttered. That was what he had said… as if he had introduced himself to the deity. "What—what did you do to me?"

"I gazed into your past. I am an astromancer as well." She smiled. "You are lucky to be alive after such an encounter. I was always informed that Calamtu was one of the most unpredictable gods."

Stormbright nodded, as if in confirmation to the woman's claims, before seeing that Steel had awakened beside him. Evidently his brother hadn't missed any of what was said, as the thief's eyes were wide from disbelief.

"Calamtu," he exclaimed. "You met Calamtu in that storm! But how—how is that even possible?"

"Your brother was *called* to be a sorcerer," Shariz'lan replied in a matter-of-fact tone. "He was chosen by Calamtu—awakened, one might say. In that sense, he is like the first of us who harnessed astromancy, in a time when we were revered by our goddess Sutana. For you see, it was the gods who opened our minds to such ways of thinking. Since then we have learned to teach others this talent, but being awakened by a deity is the most poignant way to learn.

"We sorcerers call this one's *inner sense*. It is an ability which allows us to conjure and sense the magic around us. In truth, it takes many years to develop this skill to its full potential. Even then, we may only specialize in a single school of magic at a time.

"It will be many months before you discover what you are capable of. Your specialty is lightning, as well as harnessing the fury of the heavens. I can help you learn the basics. That is one of my duties here, along with being a chirurgeon for the wounded."

"But Shariz'lan," interrupted Ya'utet, "is it wise for us to accept these outsiders? They were enlisted as enemy mercenaries, and already we are talking about giving them sanctuary."

"You are right, Ya'utet. But that, too, was hardly their decision. The dungeons under Mirungel are full of horrific things, and the torture of slaves is a near-constant factor. To enlist in a war, even in service to your enemy, would seem a mercy when compared to that agony…"

Reluctantly, the Islirian nodded as the crone undid the brothers' bonds. Steel and Stormbright rubbed their wrists and ankles as Shariz'lan righted herself. "Of course, you are free to venture elsewhere if you wish. I believe the Ilgrathians are distant enough should you wish to leave. But you would be wise to accept my offer. It's no small thing to be chosen by a god, and I can see so much hidden potential in both of you."

The brothers faced one another, as if meaning to ask the question they both knew the answer to. It was only a moment before they arrived at the same, unanimous conclusion…

What started as a few days turned into weeks, and the weeks became months.

It seemed Miracor was like the ghost of some half-forgotten era. Often during their wanderings, Steel and Stormbright were hailed by its denizens, those who tended to ramshackled smithies and garden beds, the latter serving as the city's primary source of food (second to their dwindling stock of preserved meats). They discovered that the Islirians were fascinated by the odd tale of heroism, and so they began recounting their stories as slaves.

A month-and-a-half passed before they arrived at a lone, uninhabited courtyard. The section in which they stood was mostly ruined following so many battles, as it was close to the outside wall. Although the place was covered with lichen and mildew, there remained an enticing beauty to it all.

Steel moved himself close to a pair of double-doors. The portal resounded with a groan as he and his brother pressed their weight against it. The entryway didn't budge, although they presumed the wood was rotten judging by its groans. The thief changed tactics, trying his hand at picking the lock with a coil of wire he had found earlier. There came a click as if it were unlocked, but the doors remained stolidly shut.

Steel concluded that something must be propping itself against the other side.

He signaled to his brother, and the first blow came as they charged in unison. It took them several attempts before the door gave way with a crash. There before them loomed a large hall that had been left untouched by the centuries. A thick layering of dust and cobwebs smothered every surface, and heaps of debris lay scattered over the floors. Along either side there stood a number of racks and mannequins, each holding a variety of weapons and armor. The equipment, they noticed, gleamed with a bluish and steely hue, appearing like they had been newly-forged save for the dust.

Exploring further, they discovered that the doors were originally held in place by a large wooden plank. The beam had been snapped in two—a direct result of their efforts. They also noticed a number of skeletons morbidly scattered about…

"It looks like they were trying to keep someone out. Or some*thing*…" murmured Stormbright.

"Not a bad theory, but who were they protecting themselves from? The skeletons seem much too old to have fought against the Ilgrathians."

They returned with Shariz'lan. Her expression told them everything they needed to know. "This must have been one of our armories," she spoke, "a memento of when we weren't plagued by the star wraiths. It wasn't long ago that our cities were overrun by the grisly specters. That was when our curse waxed full, and we lost hundreds-of-years' worth of knowledge and understanding. Alas, we had not yet learned that silver could kill them, nor of how burning our dead could prevent them from rising."

Stormbright presented her the strange metal, which he realized was the same substance they had worked on as slaves—moonsteel. The material was said to be very strong, as its high tolerance for heat could theoretically weather a dragon's breath.

Steel found himself a new dagger and polearm, whereas Stormbright procured yet another shortsword. The rest they left for the Islirians to find.

The place was cleared of any debris festooning its interior. Floors and shelves and tables were dusted so that nary a spec remained. The outlying courtyard they fitted with mannequins, which served as effective training dummies for those who wished to practice their skill.

It wasn't long after that rumor of the armory's restoration had spread. Steel and Stormbright were quick to hone their skills, sparring with those who joined them. Within a week's time, what started as a few playful duels became a mighty gathering of men and women, all of them spectating or looking to test their strength against the light-skinned strangers.

The young sorcerer departed frequently from the crowd. Harnessing his powers proved to be difficult and tiring work; yet after many late nights of practice he realized that his concentration was fast improving. According to the sibyl he was already exceptional for his lack of experience. Even so, there was a long way for him to go before he could hope to rival the experts.

It was after one day of training that Stormbright rejoined his brother. The thief stood there poised as his opponent brandished a blade with a smirk. The expression was cut short as the youth twisted his spear following a defensive parry, the butt of it swiping along the Islirian's feet. The man was caught off guard by the blow, falling swiftly on one side.

Not more than ten seconds had passed before the match was called. Steel was the victor.

"I see that you're going harder at it than usual," said Stormbright. "Is there something bothering you?"

"Only that my opponents don't come close to beating me." Steel gripped his sparring partner's arm, hoisting the man to his feet.

"It sounds to me like you're getting cocky."

His brother didn't respond. Stormbright followed his gaze towards the edge of the ring of people, where he spotted an exceptionally fair woman stepping closer.

There was a hint of passion in his eyes as Steel surveyed the tresses of cool ebony hair falling over her face. Her skin was a smooth, dusky pigment, and her slim figure swayed between measured steps. Her eyes glimmered not unlike a pair of emeralds.

That was when her hand fell to the shortsword at her side. The blade hissed like a wary serpent as it was unsheathed and held aloft.

Steel responded by leaning casually on his spear. "So I see a woman dares to enter the ring," he said, daring to test her resolve. "Don't think I'll hold back. There isn't an Islirian here who can defeat me."

"Those are mighty words for one so young," she retorted. "They speak of a lack of experience. Tell me—how many females have you sparred with in the past?"

"None that I can say," nodded Steel, enjoying their little back-and-forth banter.

He charged forward, his polearm outstretched in a moment's notice. However, the swordswoman didn't behave as he had anticipated. She also charged, ducking under the swift movements of his spear, quicker than he could have imagined. He sidestepped and pirouetted, narrowly avoiding her blade. Steel deftly recovered, putting a fair distance between them.

It didn't last for long. The woman tried closing distance, but Steel's spear was quick enough to prevent it. Metal and wood clashed, the sound of it punctuating their deadly dance. It seemed for a time that the fight would be a stalemate, not one side giving to another.

That was when Steel faltered; he was so distracted by his opponent's movements that he didn't notice himself moving backwards. The solid form of a mannequin met his back, startling him and shattering his focus.

The thin edge of a blade met his throat. Already she had taken advantage of the situation, her eyes glowing with feverish abandon.

"It's unwise to underestimate your opponent," she smiled.

Steel swallowed nervously. "I get your point."

The young woman took a few steps back, the other withdrawing his spear. "I believe a formal introduction is in place," she said. "My name is Kitala. I am the Queen of Miracor and Divnarost."

Steel found himself dumbstruck as the surrounding Islirians knelt before her. He and Stormbright did the same. "My name is Steel," he said. "Had I known that I would be sparring with royalty, I might have taken a bit more care in showing the proper courtesy."

Queen Kitala smiled. "And that's why I didn't say anything sooner. The word of authority doesn't carry as much weight around these parts. It takes cunning and a strong sword-arm to keep us together—especially when faced with Alcaron on one side and the star wraiths on another.

"And besides," she added, "I always relish the chance to practice."

Night fell over the city, and Zirvonia's twin-moons once again revealed themselves. The brothers joined the Islirians in gazing upon the stars, which was always their custom in their worship of Sutana. Even though their faith had diminished over the last hundred years, it was practiced all the same.

Many drinks were passed around and a wealth of stories shared, but eventually the laughter and conversation waned. A number of firepits brightened the abandoned streets about them. The silence remained supreme.

"Master Shariz'lan," began Stormbright. "My brother and I can tell that you are a wise and generous people. We've heard you speak about this curse from before, not to mention how we dealt with the creatures ourselves. Please, tell us how you were afflicted by it. I can't imagine how any of you would be deserving of such misery."

The sibyl turned, regarding the youth with a stare. "What has brought you to ask such a question?"

"Two years ago, we were little more than slaves ourselves. You and your people have shown us kindness where no one else has, save for Trilgar and Aedas. This is one of the few places that reminds me of home. We can't let you be destroyed like we were. We *won't* let that happen. Steel and I have spoken at length these last several weeks, and if there is a way we could help save you from Alcaron and these star wraiths, we will do so."

"You cannot help us," she replied. "Our crimes against Sutana are too great, and even now She forsakes us for what we've done. The Ilgrathians will be back in time, and whether or not they bring a second wave of demons at their side, we will be outnumbered regardless."

"Is there no other way we can fight back? Couldn't we use the star wraiths outside the city walls to our advantage?"

"There are some out there," she replied, "but not enough to combat an army of several thousand."

"Is there no other way?" he prodded.

A long moment passed before Shariz'lan spoke again. "At one time our sorcerers were powerful in their knowledge, but they passed into wickedness, and a great anger began to smolder inside their hearts. It was through this that they sealed their doom—as well as our own. I do not know what they did exactly, but *something* happened in our capital city—something evil that brought about our goddess' fury.

"We were aware of how our king desired to control the star wraiths, the same beings who rose up following our deaths. An artifact was created to do just that, one housing a powerful spirit that could bend reality to its whim—command all manner of spirits from the Great Beyond. We of Divnarost know this as the Oubal Staff, a magic fetish whose name is a curse to us."

Stormbright pondered for a moment. "If that is true, then how is it your ancestors didn't overcome this plague, and banish the star wraiths for good?"

"I do not know. I can only imagine that the stave is either lost or hidden. It is said that it was last seen in the lost city of Talacor, at the keep ruled by King Telinor. Queen Kitala and I have sent many to try and reclaim the relic. All of them failed."

"They are demons," interjected Kitala, who until now was making the odd flirtation with Steel. All manner of joy left as her expression hardened, eyes burning with intensity. "King Telinor was once my grandfather, but it's rumored that he leads the hordes of star wraiths against us. If that is true," her voice became colder, "then I wouldn't hesitate to cleave him apart with a silvered blade…"

"That doesn't frighten me," boasted Steel. "My brother and I shall retrieve this device, and rid you of the curse and Alcaron in a single fell swoop. We will rally all of the star wraiths and bring them against the Ilgrathians. Perhaps it will even bring the demons to heel should they be summoned again." He looked to his brother, seeing that his sentiment was a shared one.

He added, "I'm willing to bet they don't like magic. At least from what I heard of Ya'utet recounting the battle, it seems they scurried off whenever Stormbright unleashed his lightning."

"But surely you cannot fathom the dangers of this quest…" muttered Shariz'lan.

"I agree," said Kitala. "That is why *I* will be coming with you."

"But my Queen, the lands outside the city are fraught with danger, and you haven't ventured outside for such a long time. Think of how your people would react should you perish."

"We will all perish if nothing is done with these Ilgrathians," she said. "We are fortunate they haven't returned already. But they *will* be back, of that I'm certain. As for Talacor, it is a city of strange magicks, and from what I've read of the old texts, there should be a secret entrance leading into the citadel. That should give us some advantage after our last few attempts. It's a path that's easily overlooked, but I myself know the way.

"In the meantime, you and Ya'utet shall see to it that Miracor is kept safe. Your visions have allowed us to survive more than my leadership ever could, Shariz'lan. And as for Ya'utet, we have already discussed how he will lead our military. He has the people's trust, as well as my own."

The sibyl stood there in a moment of perplexity. "Aye," she muttered.

The Queen smiled. "It is settled then. Come morning, the three of us shall make our departure from Miracor. Provisions shall be arranged for us in the meantime. As for you, Steel and Stormbright, I ask that you prepare yourselves for this journey. You will need the rest."

"You speak like we won't be traveling by the road," murmured Stormbright.

"You are right, my friend. Our quest requires that we move with full speed; and for that, my artificers have devised a method of traveling through the skies. They are intelligent men—not unlike yourselves—and they should grant us the time we so desperately need."

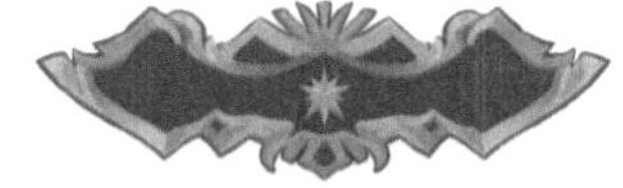

VIII
Journey Through the Sky

The sun rose overhead while Steel and Stormbright followed Kitala, with Shariz'lan at their side. Though their awakening was earlier than usual, the brothers were nevertheless thrilled by the prospects of adventure. The Queen and sibyl guided them onward with a fiery brand, one that pierced the gloom of the silent streets.

The two found their jaws dropping as they rounded a bend, spotting the domed palace which lay over a hundred cubits out from them. Alone it stood over a high-walled courtyard, as it marked itself the crowning jewel of Miracor. The brothers had espied the structure several times previously, but they were now being ushered there with full haste.

They entered through a central portico, as well as a pair of large doors. The adjoining passages were wide and lit by braziers cascading along the vast unending hallways. However, the darkness remained supreme as the torch of Shariz'lan kept them from tripping over one another. Only she and the Queen remained undisturbed in their gait, as they had traveled these halls many times before.

They emerged into a larger chamber. Steel conjectured that they must have been near the easternmost wing of the complex. The west seemed unlikely due to his trained sense of direction. The room in which they stood was circular in shape, the walls rising high above them and forming into a concave canopy overhead. A number of window-like slits filtered the morning light, their surroundings no longer obfuscated by the shadows.

Many hooded figures strode back and forth among that twilit chamber. Their appearances were quite odd at first glance, for they wore leather masks that were adorned with a pair of goggles over the eyes. The artificers would alternate from their machines towards several desks full of unfurled parchment, wherewith they would scrawl with alacrity.

Often there came an explosion of light, which caused the brothers to reel at first. They recovered their eyesight, however, as they found that neither were harmed by the experiments.

"Greetings, my Queen," said one artificer as he approached, behaving elegantly despite his appearance and muffled voice. "I'm surprised to see you and Shariz'lan here at such an early hour. What brings you and your companions to the artificer's workshop?"

"A lovely morning to you as well, Graal. We come to ask if you would lend us access to your *Heavens Barge* device. My friends and I require swift passage to Talacor, and I believe the vessel should provide the fastest means of travel."

"Yes, Your Grace," he replied. "I'm sure you're well aware that the skies are patrolled by star wraiths. There have also been other shadows we've spotted at night. They are much larger than any specter we've encountered before, and we're not entirely sure what they are."

"It is nothing we cannot handle," she said. "Our quest requires that we be as quick as possible in our travels. And from what I hear, the *Heavens Barge* is capable of just that. Besides, danger is at our doorstep no matter the path we choose. My friends and I are aware of the risks and we accept them."

Stormbright took a wary step forward, his voice tinged with fear. "What sort of creatures are these?"

"Like I said, we aren't exactly sure," replied the artificer. "We haven't encountered them ourselves, although our scouts have reported strange howlings that have echoed through the night. I cannot attest to these rumors myself, but I don't doubt their veracity."

The Islirian took a step closer. "I must warn you that this device is in its prototype stage. We've rediscovered much since the collapse of our nation, but we are only beginning to recover the knowledge we once had."

The artificer led them to an untended corner of the chamber. There the brothers saw that an array of tarps were draped over a large nondescript object, one which stood at nearly four times their own height. The coverings were removed. What lay underneath was a device they never would have imagined, not even in their wildest dreams.

The machine appeared exceedingly archaic in its design, as a metallic, basket-like perch lay underneath a plethora of valves, conduits, levers, and cranks, all of which converged at a crystalline orb above it. The light glimmering beneath its surface was not unlike the magic star towers the brothers had encountered previously.

Steel and Stormbright took a cautious step backward, as they knew well what this machine was capable of.

The Islirian covered the orb with the tarp, binding it tight so that no light seeped through. "If you are to travel the skies without being seen," he said, "it would be best that you keep the crystal covered. We have just cracked the code of making it fly, although there is much work to be done before it can be deemed safe. We artificers call it the *Heavens Barge*, specifically for its ability to coast among the stars."

"A cute name for such a tiny vessel," remarked Steel. "You sure it will hold all of us?"

"Do not worry, friend," he replied. "I can assure you that from a structural point of view it is quite sound."

"Then it will have to do," said Shariz'lan, who until this point had remained silent during the conversation.

The vessel was carried by a number of masked figures and led through a nearby doorway. The others followed suit, arriving at a large adjoining balcony. The sun had risen well above the horizon, and the glimmer of the stars had nearly faded. Only the dim reflection of Zirvonia's twin-moons could be seen, and even they were swiftly disappearing.

Seating aboard the *Heavens Barge* proved to be difficult, but luckily Steel, Stormbright, and Kitala found a suitable arrangement that could be maintained for hours at a time. The artificer instructed the trio on how they would pilot the vessel, and before long they found themselves inspecting the myriad controls at their disposal. Apparently, turning one of the dials near the orb powered the device, the vessel hissing and rising naturally as a result. Adjusting a nearby crank controlled the barge's rate of ascent (or descent), and a small wheel guided the pair of fins on either side of the stern, providing a slight jolt as one steered the craft.

"You must keep to the winds, and let the sun and stars be your guide when navigating," said Graal. "Otherwise, you risk damaging the *Heavens Barge* or getting lost. If you find that you

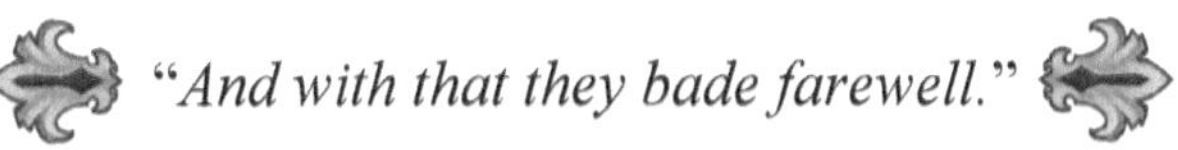

"And with that they bade farewell."

must go against the current, lower your altitude and keep as close to the ground as possible."

Once they acquainted themselves with the ship, Shariz'lan stepped forward, bowing deeply. "I am honored that you three should take on a noble quest for the sake of our people. I will pray to Sutana that you return safely."

Steel and Stormbright bowed as Kitala kept silent. "Please, don't worry for us," said Stormbright. "I swear the people of this city will know peace once again."

And with that they bade farewell. Steel was the first to man the pilot's seat. He turned the dial, and the orb beneath the tarp flashed with a sudden, albeit faint glimmer. They were slowly rising, and the city became smaller as the winds tugged the *Heavens Barge* in an easterly direction. The thief steered the vessel so it pivoted southeast.

Before they knew it, Miracor was little more than a shadow along the horizon.

The following days were slow in passing. However, the two brothers and Kitala were quick to make progress over the barren landscape. It wasn't long before they crossed the high-reaching cliff-edge that bordered the sea, and beyond they found clear skies coupled with water surrounding them on all sides.

After a time they spotted several gigantic shadows looming over the ship. Steel and Stormbright thought they were in an ambush, no less by the self-same creatures that the artificer had spoken of. The reality proved far less dangerous, as they realized that the shadows were, in fact, floating islands.

Queen Kitala looked stolidly onward, as each of the landmasses bore tendrils along their sides, diving deep into the ocean below. These, as she informed the two brothers, were vines which anchored the floating islands from further ascent. They had been raised by the Islirians in ages past. Not only had their race experimented with astromancy (the art of divination), but also geomancy (earth) and oneiromancy (reality). This allowed their magicians to conjure flora that would absorb the salt of the sea, as well as bringing freshwater to the islands.

"They are wondrous creations," murmured Stormbright, his mouth agape in a state of awe. "If we weren't on a quest to save Miracor, I would have liked to explore these islands."

"And perhaps you shall one day," said Kitala cheerfully. "It is a goal I've always had, myself—to witness the very heights of our civilization ere its end."

Further onward they spotted a network of bridges constructed of a dark, glittering metal. It was a veritable spider's web of connections between the islands. The young sorcerer appreciated their uncanny elegance, as they were even more beautiful than the capital city of the Ilgrathians.

Even so, there was a tragic aura to the awesome vista, as the structures stood lifeless and untended for decades. He turned away from it, a sorrowful mood stealing over him.

Dusk fell. Following their respite, Steel resumed his role as *de facto* pilot of the flying vessel. His course was unclear, as neither Taldriath or Bruann dared to show themselves among the night sky. A thick blanket of clouds obscured their hazy surroundings.

There a short distance from him slept Kitala, her slim silhouette almost camouflaged by night, as she lay next to a meditating Stormbright (a practice all too common for sorcerers-in-training). For the young thief, the former appeared all the more elegant and deadly, even while resting.

Her eyes opened, curiously flickering towards him.

"Trouble sleeping?" he said.

She combed the side of her hair with a hand, half of her face being distinguished among the gloom. "So it would seem. My dreams have troubled me these last few nights. I fear we are getting close."

"I'm glad," he said, before catching his own faux pas. "I mean—that's good we're getting close to the end of our quest. Not the nightmares or star wraiths, of course…"

"Of course." She giggled lightly, and for a moment it seemed Kitala's melancholy mood had left her. "Tell me, do you ever miss home? What it would have been like had everything remained the same, and you and your brother weren't taken as slaves."

"I do sometimes… though I try not to think about it much." His expression hardened. "What's done is done, and there's nothing my brother and I can do to change it. I haven't forgotten what General Caerst did to my people. What she's still doing to our father. Before the end, she *will* know what it means to have crossed us."

Kitala smiled. "A man after my own heart," she said.

Steel grinned as well, and for a moment there was an exchange of longing between them. This was halted, however, as something brought the hairs of his nape to stand on edge.

Stormbright stirred from his trance; he faced his brother and Kitala with a mixture of fear and weariness.

"Something is approaching," he said.

"We know."

A deafening groan shook the air about them. Steel withdrew his spear as Stormbright focused, conjuring an orb of lightning into existence. Kitala unsheathed her shortsword and produced a small pouch, quickly coating her blade with silvery powder.

"It is likely there are star wraiths lurking about," she said. "Be certain to rub silver dust on your weapons."

The thief did so, though Stormbright was content with focusing on his magic. It wasn't a moment after that a voluminous shadow passed by overhead. Something dislodged itself from above. A weird splattering sound met their ears, and looking up they saw a strange bulbous form had perched itself atop the *Heavens Barge*.

With a sickening motion, it slid along the side of the orb towards Steel, remaining as if it were glued to that spot! The thief didn't hesitate before plunging his spear into the thing, casting it aside within the vessel's basket.

A squeal emitted from the creature as Steel stabbed again. Finally its movements faltered, with it lying still like half-melted butter.

Moving closer to the listless mass of flesh before them, the brothers felt a sudden wave of nausea overcome them both. What was there showed more than a few similarities to the Islirians they had come to know, yet it remained as a stark perversion of all that was sane, as only the agonized features of a face could be discerned.

Shockingly enough, it seemed that an Islirian had been *merged* with this thing. Melted to conform to its distorted sense of life…

"Don't tell me this is the work of star wraiths," Steel muttered, pushing the thing over the side with his spear.

"I cannot say for certain, though I doubt it," replied Kitala, a hint of disgust stealing over her. "It's unlike anything I've ever seen before."

It was then that the larger shape passed overhead. This time Stormbright refocused the orb of energy he had created, hurling it out towards the blackened night. There he saw a hide of jet-black scales, along with a jagged spine that pierced out along its wretched form.

There came another splattering sound, as two more of the gibbering things fell onto the *Heavens Barge*. Steel was quick to dispose of the first, while Kitala slashed the latter to ribbons with her blade.

"I believe these creatures are nightmare-kin," she panted, "though I never thought the old legends were true. It's said they hail from the Nightmare Realms beyond our world—somewhere past the Great Beyond, even. Apparently, they crave the flesh of living creatures above all else."

"They look real enough to me," remarked Steel. "How do we kill them?"

Kitala looked up to the strange flying creature above. "That one I would imagine is an Oun'arc—a carrier of the fiendish devils. Try focusing your fire there!"

Stormbright took another step forward. Holding out his hands, the others saw that a lance of lightning energy was forming within them. He hoisted the projectile over his shoulder, ready to launch it at a moment's notice.

He hesitated.

"I can't see in this darkness."

"Damn it all! Let me be your eyes, then," said Steel.

A short time passed in complete silence, the three remaining on their guard. After what seemed like an eternity of waiting, the shadow of the Oun'arc emerged.

"There!!"

Stormbright launched the javelin, the projectile careening through the void without signs of slowing. The lance exploded in an instant, cascading in a dozen tendrils of electricity alongside the nightmare creature. The beast reeled as it writhed in pain. Before the trio could ready another volley of attacks, however, they realized its sounds were becoming fainter as the distance between man and monster grew.

The sorcerer leaned against the side of their ship, before settling himself down to a sitting position. "It seems I won't be having any rest tonight."

"You can count me in on that as well," Steel added.

"That makes three of us," said Kitala.

IX

The Wraith Stronghold

The trio found no rest that night, with the next day passing them almost in its entirety. They guided their ship forward, though it was evident that the Oun'arc had no intentions of returning.

The sun sank low along the horizon. This time Steel and Stormbright heard a strange howling which echoed along the wind. Queen Kitala brooded silently beside them, as they were once again enshrouded by darkness.

They were close to Talacor—that strange city of star wraiths—with its massive silhouette looming in the distance.

Spotting it from afar, they could see blackened metal adorning itself along walls of gray basaltic stone. The barrier must have risen at least fifty cubits over them. The massive keeps and tall-reaching spires towered high above.

"We are supposed to find the Oubal Staff in *there*?" Steel asked in bewilderment.

"We will just have to choose our path carefully," replied Kitala. "Since I was a child, I've heard tales of what my ancestors were capable of. Not even my wildest dreams could have prepared me for this. Rest assured, there is another way inside."

Both brothers looked at her in disbelief, as they saw that thousands of the star wraiths were moving in and out of the main gates. Many were also flying over from above, their illusory forms shifting along the heavens. Their presence gave the surrounding dusk a strange and otherworldly quality, which served to exacerbate the twain's fears.

It was as if a shroud of cosmic apparitions poured over the city walls. Wispy shapes distorted the known world into something else entirely—a momentary glimpse into the wider universe, populated by vast areas of space, streaking comets, and vibrant nebulae.

Viewed from this lens, Talacor seemed as if it were half a city. The rest of it was being devoured by the cosmos itself.

Queen Kitala sighed. "Apparently, there is an entrance my grandfather had built in ages past. If we scour the perimeter of the main wall and keep ourselves at a low altitude, then I believe the star wraiths shouldn't spot us. With any luck, the way will be made clear, assuming we search thoroughly enough."

"How do we know the side entrance is actually there?" queried Stormbright.

"As I said before, I read about it in the old texts archived by our people. It was a design written by Talacor's architect. I know it's a gamble, as we're not sure if the entrance has been obstructed since then. Still, I can see no better alternative in front of us."

"Very well," he acquiesced, turning to face the desolate ruin.

The *Heavens Barge* rapidly closed distance. Steel slowed the ship's speed as it descended, turning starboard so that the vessel and walls ran parallel. It seemed the night was on their side, for the places not frequented by star wraiths were all covered in shadow. Stormbright could barely spot his own hand in front of him, and he held no envy towards his brother's role in piloting.

There came the wails of those phantasmagoric figures from overhead, the wraiths scanning for any signs of intruders.

Even so, the trio remained hidden. Following several minutes, they found a part of the wall which bent sharply, the thief slowing the *Heavens Barge* even more so.

There before them was a small landing platform—hidden and abandoned.

The task of landing took a great amount of care, but eventually, they were relieved to feel a sense of constancy underneath their feet. Along with it came a terrible sense of vertigo. The three adventurers steadied their senses, and soon their balance returned.

They saw that an arched gateway loomed before them. And although the double-doors remained staunchly shut and locked to outsiders, Steel found little trouble in picking the lock with a coil of wire from his pack. The tumblers jostled into place with each precise movement, the spring giving little resistance as it turned… *click!*

"It seems we've found our secret entrance," murmured Stormbright. "How close are we to the central palace?"

"I'm not entirely sure," said Kitala, "but I would assume it's some distance farther still. The way should be simple and the road straight enough—assuming we don't become lost, that is."

"Let's hope you are right."

Thus Steel, Stormbright, and Kitala slipped through the opening. They fanned out separately, though they kept close to the shadows about them.

Lucky for them, it seemed that the adjoining courtyard was completely deserted. At the far end rose a manse with walls made of an ivy-stricken stone. Alas, there was no way that marked an exit, save for the one entrance leading into the lonesome estate.

After a few moments of fruitless searching, the trio inched along a path that was flanked on either side by cypresses. To Steel's surprise, the entrance was neither locked nor trapped, nor were there any strange sounds as they ventured forward. Their footsteps echoed loudly amidst the silence, and it became clear that something was wrong.

"Be on your guard," whispered Kitala, her hand moving over the pommel of her blade. Steel positioned himself at the forefront of the group, with Kitala keeping close watch behind and Stormbright heading up the rear.

There was a strange quality to the wide and opulent halls as the trio passed them through. All around them lay rooms full of gold, gems, and riches, all of the finest sort, as well as tapestries that displayed figures communing with the stars. The chambers remained suspiciously unguarded, and even the woven images seemed to leer at them as Steel and Stormbright availed themselves of the surrounding treasure.

Queen Kitala stood unperturbed, as she studied closely those hanging decorations.

"There is something familiar about this place," she said. "The hangings are much like the ones we have in Miracor's palace. Perhaps this was one of King Telinor's hidden retreats?"

The feelings of wonder faded as they continued. The halls forked in a number of strange and winding directions, with much of it defying any consistent layout known to humans or Islirians.

They lost sight of their point of entry, and after what seemed like hours of aimless wandering, Steel and Stormbright were halted by Kitala. "I'm getting the feeling we're in a trap," she said. "There must be some way that leads to an exit—unless there isn't one here at all."

Steel added: "I get the same feeling. I can't tell how this place is turning us around so much."

For a moment they stood there, trapped in a state of frustration as they postulated. It was then that Stormbright emerged from his ruminations, snapping his fingers with a laugh.

"Of course!" he exclaimed. "How did I not see it earlier, especially after what Shariz'lan taught me about illusions?"

"Illusions?" inquired Steel.

The youth held out his hands as he motioned them along one corridor. It came to a dead end, however Stormbright did not falter as he continued forward.

"You are moving into a wall, Stormbright." Kitala reached out to stop him, before noticing the sorcerer had disappeared behind its surface. He vanished, as if he were formless and immaterial like a star wraith.

A moment passed before Stormbright returned. The youth phased through the strange non-substance of the wall, a smirk spreading across his adolescent face. "It's an illusion made by magic," he said. "I sensed that something was wrong about this place—like a strange itching sensation in the back of my mind— but I didn't think of it until now. The magic is clear to me. I can *see* the illusions around us. There are several walls like this one that run along both ways." He pointed back to where he had disappeared. "I believe the exit should be around the next corner, actually."

"That would explain a lot of things," Steel nodded in reply. "But what about the treasure and the art pieces we found?"

"I don't doubt they are illusions as well." He examined the gold and gems they had procured. For a moment he ran his fingers along them, and it seemed that a small current passed through each object. The realization dawned on them that the gold was little more than a bunch of lead coins. The gems, likewise, were just tiny lumps of the same material.

"Well that's disheartening," murmured Steel, who held out his own treasure and handed it to his brother, realizing it was also lead. "We've been duped with these worthless baubles!"

"At the very least we know our way out," Kitala interjected. "I do not doubt these were made to trick and turn away trespassers. Either way, I leave my faith unto you, Stormbright. Lead on."

The youth nodded, as they once again passed through the illusory wall. There on the other side Stormbright, Steel, and Kitala saw that the hall continued like it had before. Rounding another corner, the room opened into a large ruined foyer, albeit remarkably well-kept for its age. A set of double-doors were positioned along the far wall, which the trio realized was the exit.

"And here I was thinking we had seen everything."

"Sadly not, my friend," said Kitala. "In fact, I fear more is yet to come."

Passing quietly through the doors, they found that the streets were bereft of any and all life. The road curved in helter-skelter fashion as they continued, their footsteps magnified by the emptiness around them. They knew that the hordes of star wraiths were still out there, though it was uncertain why their way was clear.

Further along they found an aged portcullis looming over them. It was evident that the gate hadn't been used for some time, as much of it was firmly rusted in place.

"It looks like the damn thing is sealed tight," Steel cursed. "Even if we were capable of opening it, the turn crank is on the other side."

Kitala turned her gaze above, shrugging. "It seems we'll have to climb then."

The swordswoman took a couple steps back, before dashing and leaping at a nearby relief. Her arms moved with surprising dexterity, and it wasn't long before the Queen of Divnarost had hauled herself atop one of the parapets.

Another second went by before the brothers saw a length of rope falling at their feet. The thief was first to haul himself up, being followed closely by the sorcerer. Kitala retrieved the rope, looping it once more in a coil before stashing it within her bag. They crept down a stair which lay on the other side.

Talacor Keep stood before them.

"I can't believe we haven't spotted any more star wraiths," murmured Steel.

Stormbright pondered while reaching out with his wizardly *inner sense*. "Be that as it may, I can tell we are being watched."

Pushing the doors slightly ajar, the trio slipped inside with nary a sound to their movements. The way behind closed just as noiselessly, and then they were engulfed by darkness.

Their vision readjusted as they felt along the walls and floor of the wide-spanning hallway. Following several minutes of silence, they came to an arched threshold that glowed with natural light.

Of all the places Steel and Stormbright had ever encountered within their lives, none of them compared to the sheer majesty of what lay before them. At first glance, the chamber appeared as if it was constructed by giants—or perhaps their ancestors—as the trio were dwarfed in size by massive walls spanning an infinity above. The stonework about them lay embossed with past tales of glory— bas reliefs showing the rising of great islands unto the skies, as well as those hinting at battles won by massive aerial ships.

"This must be a record of the floating islands," whispered Stormbright.

Kitala nodded. "They also show our history with airships. How they darkened the very skies with their presence…"

"*Airships?!*" spoke Steel in bewilderment.

"Did you think ours were the first? No—what we have is a rough imitation, at least compared to what we were once capable of building."

A number of archways loomed alongside each wall, as they offered a lofty view over the city. Stormbright could only imagine what this place must have looked like one-hundred years ago, back when the Islirians were at the peak of their might…

He faced the center of the chamber. Before them spanned a scarlet rug which climbed up a series of steps. The massive structure supporting it was a ziggurat, defined by the same black marble as the rest of the room. Its top was flat, however, as a lone seat lay perched on its surface.

A short distance next to it hovered a sprite, one they recognized as a star wraith. The specter appeared more regal as a crown lay atop its head. In one of its appendages there was a long haft of metal, a staff that was curved and pointed in the shape of an elongated "S."

"So you've succeeded in finding me," a voice boomed with a sonorous tenor. "I welcome you to the palace of Talacor. Tell me, do you seek the Oubal Staff? Or is it perhaps my soul you wish to claim?"

"We are here for both!" Kitala shouted as she drew her blade lined with silver dust. Though a vast distance spanned between both parties, the Queen of Miracor moved with a speed that would have surprised her. She climbed the steps and struck vigorously with her weapon. The ghost of King Telinor was quick to dodge; the wraith shifted to one side, rearing up the butt end of the Oubal staff, clobbering the Islirian and bringing her to her knees.

For a split second, Steel and Stormbright remained stationary, before they, too, readied themselves. The former leveled his spear, whereas lightning flashed in the space between Stormbright's hands. A stream of electricity shot forth, causing the form of the star wraith to shudder violently as a result.

Steel was quick to follow this, as he charged forward and upward, a sequence of stabs revealing a number of holes in the starry veil that was his enemy. The star wraith shifted and stretched, as if it would drain the life out of Steel, but it was quickly countered by a swipe from Kitala's weapon, dealing it a grievous wound in the process.

She returned to her feet and stood over the form of King Telinor, holding her blade to what she imagined was the throat of the specter.

"At last, my time has come," said the wraith, its words losing none of their potency. "For the sake of my people, I shall gladly embrace death."

Kitala hesitated for a moment, though her blade was outstretched, poised for the killing. "Not yet," she said coldly. "I have questions that need answering. *Do you know who I am?*"

"You are my granddaughter," replied the wraith, as if it had known that fact all along.

"And do you know why we came here for the Oubal Staff?"

The star wraith nodded its amorphous head. "Aye. But know that your quest will be a fruitless one. You cannot hope to control us. Not even I could do so without being corrupted by the taint of our curse."

"And why is that?" The Queen's eyebrow raised by a hair.

"It's because we aren't a species from the Great Beyond. I cannot hope to explain the nature of our curse, but we are something different than what you think. Even if I could control my brethren with the staff, I know it has a will of its own. It has always denied my attempts to use it; none of us could have foreseen that it would resist our efforts after we made it."

"I will not tolerate your lies!" Kitala raised her blade, before it was caught mid-swing by Stormbright.

"He is not lying!" the youth shouted, forcing her arm down to her side. "Though I struggle to believe it myself, there is a hint of truth in what he says. When I fought with the star wraiths outside Miracor, I sensed an odd intelligence within them, though I didn't recognize it at the time. If what your grandfather says is true, then these creatures aren't ghosts or demons, but something else entirely… Perhaps even a new and intelligent race."

Kitala hesitated, before shaking her arm free from the sorcerer. She sheathed her blade, facing the starry form of King Telinor.

"Very well. According to my companion you have spoken to us truthfully, and his words I trust. Tell me more, then, about this Oubal Staff. Why do you hold it? How is it that the stave defies your will?"

The star wraith collected itself, though it was clearly shaken by its wounds. "The Oubal Staff is a relic of our people. Even though I cannot wield it, it is the symbol of Divnarost's King. As for the nature of why it resists me, it's because the spirit inside knows we are weak and cannot control it. It mocks us for creating the curse, as in time we, too, fell victim to its influence. Only I was spared by the staff, at least my mind, so that I might witness the horror of my legacy. The rest of us were driven mad as our memories of life became fragmented. We were consumed by an uncontrollable hatred. Thus it holds us in contempt, as it will only aid those it deems worthy."

"Wait a moment," said the thief. "You said that your sorcerers created the curse?"

"Indeed," replied King Telinor, "as well as myself. It's most fitting that I should join my brothers in its cold embrace, as it has forever scarred our people. The curse was a product of our lust for immortality, not to mention our desperation to repel the nightmare-kin who threatened us.

"We were foolish, as we thought that we could hold together as one mind. The spells my sorcerers weaved made us each immortal, immune to the chaotic influence the eldritch monstrosities held over us. However, those of us who turned into wraiths began destroying each other. Our ego proved to be our downfall, and ever since, death has walked at our heels.

"I cannot ask for you to forgive us—forgive me—for what we have done. Our crimes are too great. Do what you must—end my life—for my mind has lingered since on the prospect of death."

A moment passed before Kitala replied: "I will not kill you. There is one last duty you must fulfill. To the north, the kingdom of Alcaron invades my country and threatens to enslave our people. If possible, I would have my friend Stormbright wield the Oubal Staff against them. If you can teach him how he might do so, then perhaps we shall succeed where you have failed."

The sorcerer inched closer to the star wraith. "As for you and the others," he said, "I may not be able to control you, but that is fine with me. I wouldn't wish to command you anyway. Instead, I ask that you aid us in repelling these invaders."

"What?!" Kitala faced the youth, her face one of shock.

Stormbright shrugged his shoulders. "Perhaps he could help us and atone for his sins. We have nothing left to lose, anyway. I can sense that there's some air of authority about him. The other star wraiths may well listen to his commands if he decides to work with us."

"Perhaps you are right," she acceded. "King Telinor—er, grandfather—why is it we weren't attacked on the way here? Surely there must have been a reason…"

The star wraith eyed them closely through slitted eyes. "Even from afar, I could sense that one from my bloodline was drawing close. I guess you could say I wished to look upon your face before I met my demise." He turned slightly, his expression one of guilt. "I called off my brethren to see you in the flesh. Now I can see that you are my granddaughter, and even after one-hundred years of war, you have shown yourself to be a mighty and suitable heir."

The wraith shimmered as he continued. "But I can tell there is something more between us. I sense it; even my subjects around me feel the same…"

The trio saw that a number of star wraiths were emerging from the nearby balconies, filtering in by the formless dozens.

"We wish to learn from you, remember what it was once like to have memories that aren't fragmented. If that means saving what's left of the Islirians, then we will do so."

Kitala smiled. "Perhaps there is hope for us after all. We can try to study the curse, see if there's a way we can overcome it. It may take some time, but at the very least it should help mend the gap between us."

The king of the star wraiths turned back to his fellow cohorts, then to the three adventurers.

"We accept your offer," he said. "Lead onwards."

X

A Hasty Retreat

The trio accompanied the star wraith, passing through the entrance to Talacor Keep.

A host of specters was gathering about them, an army which numbered in the thousands. The star wraiths gazed thoughtfully in their direction, although there was no unwanted movement as King Telinor gestured with a shadowy hand.

Two figures emerged from the assembly, cranking at the rusted gate which stood before them. The portcullis shrieked open, rising inexorably upward…

"Your earlier speculations were correct, Stormbright. So long as I'm in the company of my fellow star wraiths, they will follow my commands as if I were king of Divnarost. Even though I cannot harness the Oubal Staff, there is still some measure of obedience among my subjects."

Stormbright gazed along either side as they traveled further. He could sense a torrent of wild emotions coming from those around him—a hint of intelligence and individuality that was being rediscovered.

He couldn't help but pity them.

"How will you and your star wraiths be joining us?" he interjected, halting at the manse they had snuck through earlier. "We ventured here atop a small flying vessel ourselves, a ship we've since referred to as the *Heavens Barge*. Surely you must have required something similar, at least when you were alive."

"That we did, though we haven't needed it for some time after we learned how to fly. My brethren and I will accompany you as we are; yet if you wish it so, you may be granted passage aboard one of our ships. It is a quick and speedy vessel, and I would presume it's much faster than this '*Heavens Barge*' of which you speak."

The trio turned to one another, their moods in agreement. "We accept," replied Steel. "Though our ship is usable, it is also quite small. Besides, the extra speed should save us a few days on our return trip." He pondered for a moment. "Still, I think there's value in us keeping it. Would it be possible to land our vessel aboard yours?"

"I have no qualms with it, myself," the star wraith nodded. "If there is nothing else for us to speak about, I will meet you there shortly. Look to the skies above the city and you will spot us soon enough." King Telinor turned away from them, addressing the hundreds of specters who stood behind. There was no sound in his words, but the star wraiths stirred as if responding to an urgent series of commands.

The three adventurers departed from the gathering. They emerged through the courtyard on the other side, finding that the *Heavens Barge* had been largely untouched since their initial landing. The machine gave a shuddering groan as it restarted and ascended once more. Steel turned the vessel so its driving fins caught the currents of wind. The buoyancy of the crystal orb brought them higher, as they were presented with a bird's-eye view of the metropolis.

Once they had reached a suitable distance to the northeast (as the wind also blew that way), the young thief turned the wheel, allowing the ship to float in a northwesterly direction.

They heard a thrumming from nearby, seeing that an even larger ship had arisen from the city. Its prow was slim but no less high-reaching; its mass was sleek as it coasted through the sky like a ship over water. A short distance behind flew the remainder of the star wraiths, their nameless forms coalescing in a vague shroud of starry phantasma, specked here and there with those white, pupil-less eyes.

They landed atop the other ship. Steel and Stormbright noted that the deck was largely unmanned, save for the odd specter who flitted from one end to another.

"I bid you welcome to the *High-Crester*," said King Telinor as he descended along the deck, "the most prized vessel within our fleet. It has been long since we first steered it through the heavens. The ship is a relic from when our oneiromancers were at their prime. The number of crewmen we require is very few, as levitation orbs propel the vessel beneath these very decks. We need only a driver and those who can adjust the sails. We also have ballista cannons standing at three abreast on either side."

"Truly, it's a mighty boat," murmured Stormbright. "I believe we are all thankful to be here instead of our own ship. There's so much space, and it's thrice as fast as ours."

The star wraith nodded. "Let us make haste," he said. "I sense time is of the essence."

The wind brushed against their faces as the *High-Crester* sped its way onward. It bounded without effort through clear skies, passing clouds and floating islands in a matter of minutes, towards the distant horizon beyond.

The days elapsed in similar fashion as they sped past their surroundings. Steel and Stormbright felt their spirits rising. The Oubal Staff was in their possession, and an army of star wraiths flew at their side.

It wasn't long after that the sorcerer tried reaching out to the stave, with King Telinor instructing him on how to focus his mind, practice that mysterious art of telepathy. Alas, the spirit would not respond to any of his questions—much to his and the star wraith's dismay.

By the end they were left disappointed, which furthered the seed of doubt that was beginning to grow.

Steel leaned against the railing of the ship's prow. The city of Miracor could be seen near the horizon, and they were fast approaching it. The thief focused his vision, spotting the glimmering view of moonsteel encompassing the landscape. It was the armies of Alcaron, he saw, and they had returned sooner than he expected. Before, hundreds of mercenaries had made up the majority of the force, yet it seemed that Ilgrathié was sending in Her special army of Falcons. Where the humans had failed, the noble Ilgrathians would succeed.

The hairs on the back of his neck stood rigid. *Something* was soaring in the skies overhead, and he could sense it coming towards their position!

"Everyone, get down!" he shouted. Suddenly, hundreds of scaly demons flew out from underneath, surrounding them. The airship was overwhelmed in a matter of seconds, and Steel, Stormbright, and Kitala were in a fight for their lives.

Stormbright and Kitala dashed behind a row of untended cargo. The young thief followed suit, yet not before stabbing into one of the hellions above, causing its bloodied form to fall in a heap along the deck.

"I guess we've found the welcoming party," he said as he joined them.

Nearby, Stormbright released a bolt of lightning that shot through the mighty host, reducing several more of the creatures into a smoldering black ruin.

The young sorcerer faced them both: "We will have to dispatch as many of them as we can. If the entire horde is here, then Dimorn must be close by."

Meanwhile, the star wraiths about them cleaved their way into the demonic numbers. The fiends were forced to respond, turning away from the two brothers and Kitala, as many were drained of vitality. The hellions' bodies shriveled, becoming little more than wrinkled husks. Their teeth bared in a frenzy, before the strength of their wings failed and they plummeted hundreds of cubits towards the sea below.

The specters seemed not to take any tangible form as they slew, felling dozens out of the hundreds who pressed against them. However, there emerged several holes among that shroud as their enemies fought back, the two opposing forces drawn into a stalemate.

There were fiends who sought with teeth and talons towards the brothers. The two of them sustained many wounds as they fought to stay alive, but Kitala's wits and quick sword-arm prevented them from being slain. Her blade sang with cruel efficiency, its edges doused in red while moving constantly, outwitting those who fought her with ease. In that moment of crisis, she could have easily been mistaken for a dancer, bending and pirouetting with the utmost elegance. Only the piles of dead surrounding her told them otherwise.

The brothers aided her in much the same manner, as she clashed against an army of jagged teeth and razor-sharp claws. Occasionally, they were given the precious seconds they needed to release the odd cannon shot. Whatever demons they hit were replaced, and their enemies swarmed onward and inward with ever increasing numbers.

The *High-Crester* was drenched in a veil of congealed blood and viscera, and it shuddered as the ship had become quite damaged.

It was then that the sorcerer found his moment of reprieve. Stormbright honed his senses, clearing his mind of all stimuli. He felt outward with his *inner sense*, searching for the leader of the infernal army.

There came a foreign presence to his mind, and he knew right away that the sciomancer controlling those demons was close.

He opened his eyes, spotting the shadow that passed behind the demonic forms. If he hadn't known it was his enemy in hiding, then he certainly would have missed it.

Now was his chance. The magician channeled all of his strength and mind-power into the digits of his fingers. Then, almost as if the opening was destined to be there, he found a clearing among the warring bodies. The tendrils of energy materialized in a solid projectile, which he launched like a javelin. The lightning bolt careened without slowing, as if it were bent on defying the laws of physics.

It collided with the sciomancer. The Ilgrathian shuddered and convulsed as his rukh bore him closer, halting as its wings flapped in place.

Dimorn coughed and sputtered. He was a man who had been ratted out from his hiding place.

"So the sorcerer and thief have decided to face me," he said. "You must believe me when I say you have great tenacity. But now your time has come!"

"You speak proudly for someone who shows himself in the open," retorted Steel. He raised his bow, nocking an arrow and releasing it with perfect accuracy. The rukh was quick to dodge the oncoming projectile, despite its bulky size.

Stormbright cursed in response. Of course, the sciomancer had the upper hand. His brother was only delaying the inevitable. Sooner or later the strength of the star wraiths would falter—there were simply too many demons all around them—and then they would be mere playthings for the magician.

"I must admit, you show skill for your age." He snickered. "However, we both know the odds are against you. Miracor will grow weaker before the battle is won, and even your spectral friends cannot delay it. Rather, it would be best that you give up here and now. There is nowhere to run—no Islirians to save you from being maimed and killed. Give yourselves up now and they shall be spared."

The sciomancer smiled. "I will make sure that the three of you are all well-cared for. As for this one," he pointed towards Stormbright, "you would make a most promising disciple."

"We've already experienced your version of hospitality," Steel spat at the ground. "We suffered through that hell for two years! I would sooner die before going back there."

"Indeed. Yet I wouldn't be taking you on as slaves. Rather, I aim to train you as personal assassins."

"And for what purpose is that?" Steel felt the anger rising in the back of his throat.

The sciomancer chuckled. "Why, to dispatch with Ilgrathié and General Caerst, of course. That *is* what you want, isn't it?"

A brief moment of shock hit them both, even Kitala who was fending off the hordes of demons behind them.

"But… why," spoke the sorcerer, "why would you do such a thing after serving your goddess for so long?"

"The answer is simple: I aim to overthrow Her once she's brought the world to heel. There is only one way to attain divinity, and it would require time as well as a god's blood to be possible. But it would be worth it. I could guide this world in a better direction—a place where we can be the masters of our own fate."

"All of this talk, then, just for power… Is that it?" retorted the thief.

"You don't understand," said the sciomancer. "We sorcerers serve the natural laws governing this universe, ones that are above any god or goddess. Do not think for a moment we are as rigid as General Caerst. We are a solid caste above the world. I seek lasting peace, my friends, and I know that only *I*, myself, can bring that about. You must see reason in what I'm saying. It is only natural that gods should fall and mortals will rise to take their place. Will you not join me in this noble venture?"

Stormbright stepped forward, giving a knowing glance to his brother. "Your goal isn't noble at all," he said. "Nor will we submit to your twisted sense of justice."

He dashed for the Oubal Staff, retrieving it with one hand as Steel pulled taught his shortbow, loosing several more arrows in the sciomancer's direction. Dimorn jerked the reins of his rukh, moving the great beast to one side, yet the attack wasn't made to kill, only distract.

The young magician detected a faint voice which came from the Oubal Staff. He wasn't sure why it decided to speak with him only now, at a time when both the lives of himself and his friends were at stake, but he didn't question the matter any further. He concentrated, hearing the vague murmurings of words beckoning to him, though what they were he couldn't tell.

His concentration was cut short as a sharp pain pierced through him. He saw that a javelin was jutting out from his stomach. He could feel the excruciating agony… along with a sense of coldness as his strength waned.

"No!" shouted Steel. The thief dove and cushioned Stormbright's fall while cradling his brother's head.

The sciomancer gave a hoarse, shrill laughter. He was the one who had hidden the weapon in secret, hurling it at the opportune moment in case it was needed. "So you've chosen the path of damnation and ruin," he mocked, smiling. "Look at what it has cost you! Farewell, Steel and Stormbright. Know that it was your naiveté that ended you!"

He turned to leave with his rukh, yet not before Steel got to his feet, firing one last arrow in his direction. Perhaps it was a lapse in Dimorn's awareness, as, remarkably, the missile struck true! The sorcerer growled in pain, while the infernal demons were routed by the star wraiths.

King Telinor and Kitala looked at each other, the former shimmering with disgust, before their attention was drawn towards Stormbright.

"No, Zolan…" Steel whispered as he knelt down, feeling his brother's shallow breaths. He sobbed lightly. "Don't leave me. We've got to keep fighting, we can't let them get to us! You can't die, Zolan…"

The words came to the ears of Stormbright; but he did not comprehend them. His vision was going black, and everything inside went icy cold save for the warm fluid pooling along his side.

He heard a strange purring sound as his eyes shut close. Along with it came the sensation of being pulled somewhere at a high speed, though where exactly he did not know.

"Stay with us," a voice whispered.

He fell into darkness.

XI

A Lament for Hope

"Please, Zolan. Don't leave us. Don't die on me now…"

Kitala felt the boy's neck as Steel kept his brother close, weeping softly. "There is a pulse," she said, "though it's faint. We must get him to our healers, and quickly!"

Steel made no reply. His insides swirled amidst a torrent of rage and confusion. Just the mere thought of General Caerst or Dimorn didn't fail in bringing his blood to a boil.

This couldn't be happening, he thought to himself. Not again—not after what happened to father…

"I will take him to Miracor, myself," muttered their star wraith companion, his eerie form shimmering.

"But you can't," protested Kitala. "My men and I are trained to spot star wraiths and shoot them out of the sky. You must allow me to come with you. That way you aren't torn to ribbons."

"I will not stay behind, either," added the thief, his hatred burning inside him like hot coals.

"Very well," said King Telinor. "My wraiths will take over the *High-Crester* from here. They can maneuver it near the city's edge while we depart."

The star wraith cradled Stormbright within his arms, while the other two were picked up by specters who flew alongside each other. Despite their initial hesitation, their allies' touch was harmless. The flight was an uncomfortable one, yet Steel and Kitala gritted their teeth as they saw a procession of archers drawing aim from below. Their weapons were lowered, however, as the figure of Ya'utet brought them to a stop.

"Hold your fire!" shouted the Islirian warrior. "Our Queen and the humans are among them."

Soon the star wraiths and trio landed before the host of soldiers. Ya'utet's expression was one of fright mingled with concern.

"My Queen, what is this about?" he said. "Surely, you're not in league with the star wraiths."

"Do not worry, Ya'utet. They have decided to help us against the Ilgrathians. I will explain more later. Right now, Stormbright is wounded and we require aid from Shariz'lan and our healers. Our fellow sorcerer must be tended to immediately!"

The warrior stood frozen, almost in a fit of perplexity, before nodding. "As you wish, Your Grace," he replied, turning and dashing over the ruined cobbled streets with several others.

Ya'utet returned with Shariz'lan and a half-dozen figures at his side. The young sorcerer was carried away, with Telinor departing to rejoin his fellows along the *High-Crester*.

Before long, it was Steel, Kitala, and a few Islirians left.

"He will be fine," she said. "Just have faith and be patient."

"Yeah…" Steel's voice sounded hollow as he mulled over her words. Still, the anger inside him wouldn't go away… "You know," he continued, "sometimes I wonder if we weren't cursed, ourselves. Ever since my brother spotted that meddlesome god within the storm, our lives have been nothing but one tragedy after another. The gods are toying with us—Calamtu, Sutana, Ilgrathié… all of them.”

“You can’t say such things. Look at where our defiance of Sutana has brought us! That was a product of our *own* hubris! Not that of the gods.”

“And what about myself and Stormbright?” he said, raising his voice. “What did we ever do wrong?”

Kitala opened her mouth, but nothing was said in reply.

“That’s what I thought,” he said.

Another moment passed before she continued, “Come on. We have a city to defend.”

It came as no surprise that Miracor’s defenders were in a state of panic. The few who took on the roles of leading advisers were held in a vise as to what should be done. The Queen of Divnarost became occupied in dealing with the heated bureaucracy. Meanwhile, Steel was left to scour the city, preparing for the fight that would surely come.

He found no relief as he patrolled the city wall’s perimeter, seeing that a counterattack had already taken place during their absence. The denizens of Miracor had fended off the invaders with a mixture of desperation and good luck. Even so, the ramparts and battlements were in a state of near-complete ruin, as the Ilgrathians’ new-and-improved siege engines were said to be nigh-unstoppable.

“It appears General Caerst has wisened up to our plans,” said one Islirian manning the wall. “It’s part of the curse, I tell you. A byproduct of the star wraiths who dock their wretched ship among us."

Steel learned that the man was not alone in his thoughts. Several others who fought were perplexed as to why the Queen had taken their age-old enemies as allies. Threats were hurled against him, as they realized that he had also played a role in what transpired.

He grimaced. They didn't know about the star wraiths' true nature, nor of how vital they would be in the coming conflict.

The youth was left brooding as he rejoined Kitala, who in turn was accompanied by the sibyl. It appeared they had just finished speaking with King Telinor, and that the *Heavens Barge* was returned to the balcony where they had taken to the skies. Steel learned that the other vessel at their disposal, the *High-Crester*, had been severely damaged from the fight. Several cracks spanned along its levitation crystals, and so the ship was grounded until it could be repaired.

"What news is there of my brother?" he inquired. "Does he show any signs of improvement?"

The look Shariz'lan gave him was a sullen one. "As a chirurgeon I've done all I can for the boy, but he has not woken yet. He has lost so much blood… I cannot guarantee that he will survive, Steel. I am sorry."

The thief remained silent as Kitala walked to his side. "Would you like to see him?" she asked.

"No," was his reply. "There's still too much to be done. My brother would frown if he knew I used this time to mourn for him."

Kitala began to speak, but it was already too late. The double-doors of the palace slammed shut, leaving the Queen and Shariz'lan alone.

Several hours passed before the sun touched the edge of the horizon. Steel, exhausted by his toils, had done all he could to assess the situation, seeing that each soldier was well-fitted for battle. Naturally, this led him to the armory that he and Stormbright had previously restored. His training with the other soldiers continued long into the night, one drill being issued after another. After a while, he bid that they rest with their families, as this would likely be the last time they could do so.

The number of soldiers filtered out, one-by-one, and Serithas was left alone in the courtyard. He had managed to clear his thoughts somewhat through his training with his fellow Islirians. Even so, his mind was in a state of utter disarray...

"I figured you would be here."

The youth turned, seeing it was Kitala who stood next to him. With her arrival he realized that the stars, along with Zirvonia's two moons, had revealed themselves in full splendor. The sight reminded him of the night they had first met.

That seemed so long ago...

"How are you faring?" she asked, seating herself beside him.

"Well enough, I suppose." He didn't give her any attention, so much as he regarded the stars and moons above. In them he found a strange sort of solace. However, he couldn't let its soothing influence blunt his mind's edge. He would need that for saving Miracor... lest he lose all hope.

Not a word was spoken as Kitala's arms wrapped around him. There was a comfort in her warmth, like two kindred flames finding vitality in one another. Her tresses of raven hair fell from her shoulders, brushing over his own.

The thief felt a gentle hand turning his gaze towards her. It was like a dam had been broken. His lips caressed her own, all the fury and sorrow swelling under a series of passionate kisses.

They embraced each other, and their love-making that night was gentle and fulfilling, as the moons stared on jealously from above, their hearts blazing in silent fury.

When Stormbright next awoke, he saw that the color of sky had inexplicably changed; it shone with a distinct shade of violet, as well as hints of crimson and magenta. The three pigments swirled in an oily mixture high above him, never truly coalescing.

He rose to his feet, groaning in pain.

Strangely enough, the youth's wounds had all but disappeared. Was he dead? No, something didn't feel right about it. Perhaps his mind was playing tricks on him, and he was really in some half-real, half-delirium-induced purgatory? It was at least a possibility. Still, he had no idea what this place was.

The magician surveyed his surroundings, his eyes perusing the mysterious contours of the ebony landscape. The soil, he noted, was discolored with striations of gray ash, as if there had been some type of flora growing before it was set aflame. There were places around him where a lesser flower grew. Its make was rather peculiar, as it held the essence of fire within its waving petals.

The vegetation glowed brightly, and Stormbright dared not hazard touching it.

Nevertheless, there was a cold luster to this land. Stormbright recalled once more the events that had led him here. The ambush by those demons; his encounter with the sciomancer; that spear-wound along his stomach…

He steadied himself from the sudden wave of nausea. His breath eased in tempo, as he collected himself from that haunting realization.

He wondered if it were even possible to return to his world. Only one fact remained certain: he would first have to learn more about this place before he could hope to escape.

Stormbright moved forward, finding that he had lost none of his vitality after being wounded. His mood, however, was anything but jovial, as questions of his current whereabouts dominated his mind.

His eyes flickered near and afar to discern where he might be going. Often, he found his gaze returning to the swirling vortex above. Sadly, there was no celestial body to guide his passage, only that strange foliage along the ground.

He found the going both difficult and tiring. After a while, he slackened in pace, his mood brightening when he saw the landmark which stood before him.

For all the abnormalities in that realm, the structure he spotted was even stranger. Glittering lights danced across the tower's surface as it rose hundreds of cubits in the air, cascading in a myriad branches not unlike a tree. Its boughs resembled the ash remains he had spotted earlier; its leaves were dull with a strange violet hue, and the trunk underneath was a scintillant, luminescent amber.

Deep down, Stormbright knew he would have to make his ascent if he wanted to rejoin his brother and Kitala. Luckily, there was an arched gateway that opened at the base of the structure. He shrugged his shoulders, moving himself forward and shoving the bulk of his weight onto the door's frame.

The portal gave way with a groan as he stepped inside. He was surprised to find that a path had been carved out for him. It ascended on either side at a smooth incline, looping along a landing that stood some distance overhead. He took the leftmost path, though it seemed there was little difference between the two disparate ramps.

While climbing, he peered once over the lofty precipice; the youth shuddered, instinctively taking several steps back. He had already ascended many floors, not to mention the base of the tower was a vague suggestion below.

Stormbright breathed a sigh, continuing his climb. Onward and upward he stole, as he used both his hands and feet while tirelessly scaling one level after another. With each, the angle of the ramps grew steeper, and there emerged ruinous gaps which broke up the path before him. One of these he found spanned a full ten-cubits across, with no alternate route showing itself.

Stormbright looked on with concern. He would have to cross that gap if he hoped to reach the other side…

After a moment or two of pondering, he produced a dirk from his pack. Normally daggers weren't his style, but its purpose here would be paramount, as there were many cracks along the wall that could provide sufficient purchase. There were also several footholds serving as a nice leadup to those closely-set fissures.

He held the blade with his teeth as he promptly set about the precarious climb, first grabbing one outcropping of amber above him, then another.

The sorcerer's wiry muscles strained with each movement. He dared not look down, for he knew exactly what kind of sight would await him if he did so.

Suddenly, Stormbright felt his foot slip out from underneath. His entire weight was placed under the hold of his one hand. Reflexively, he looked down, and immediately regretted it, feeling the surge of panic that came with his predicament.

Now looking to the other side, he saw that the adjoining ramp was several cubits out from him. He hadn't even reached the cracks along the wall; but perhaps he could leap the remaining distance…

What happened next he didn't fully comprehend until after the fact, but he remembered straining upward using his one arm. With the other, he retrieved the dirk from his teeth, placing his feet at about waist-level along the wall. With a swift motion he leapt towards the far precipice, driving the tip of his dagger in a crack over the edge. The amber-stuff held. He hoisted himself over, narrowly avoiding what would have been a long and deadly fall.

All of this Stormbright processed as he caught his breath in great gulps. He moved up the surface of the ramp, if for no other reason than to further the stretch between himself and that chasm of death.

Eventually, he crawled his way up to level ground, standing once again. He breathed a sigh of relief, realizing that he was at the top of the amber tower.

An archway loomed close by. Stormbright motioned himself along a platform that led outside, built atop the boughs of the amber tree. The chaotic skies swirled and churned overhead. Brushing aside the violet foliage obstructing his vision, he was in the middle of a wide clearing. A central dais rose a few steps out from him, and the throne sitting atop it was a striking ebony. Though its seat was empty, at its side was a creature the magician found most intriguing. Its form was vaguely recognizable as a lioness', yet there was a strange human quality to its face as it warily regarded him.

The feline stirred just a trifle, revealing the cloven hooves which supplanted its hind feet. Its tail rose high above its head, revealing a stinger-like barb that was akin to a scorpion's.

The sorcerer took a step back. The creature in turn relaxed, allowing its hooves and paws to fall under the mass of its bulk. It brandished a look of caution towards the youth.

"Where am I?" he asked. Stormbright wasn't even sure the beast could talk, but anything was worth trying in a place like this.

"You are in my realm," the creature mewled, its voice like a thousand souls speaking in unison. "I'm the master of all that happens here."

"*What* are you?"

"Once, I was a manticore who patrolled the boundaries of the Underworld, a place lurking along the space between worlds. You may know this as the Great Beyond. But now, I am the guardian of this staff. You may call me Oubal if you wish, for my name is no different than this prison."

The half-feline, half-human eyes squinted at him, as the purring voice of the manticore continued. "I'm guessing you are the one who tried to summon me? For a moment, I even considered aiding you in your plight. I see that your strength gave out before I could help. It appears your spirit remains here, while your body lingers at death's door."

The youth gazed at the creature in disbelief. "So I'm not dead then? Instead, I'm within some kind of realm of your creation? A realm *within* the staff?"

"Precisely," purred Oubal. "As of this moment, I could exile you if I so wanted—allow your soul to return to its body. I imagine you would first like me to heal your wounds. Otherwise you will likely perish."

Stormbright nodded, though he wasn't aware of magic being used for healing. If such methods were available, then why wasn't everyone using it?

"Why didn't you answer my pleas for help until now?"

The thing remained motionless as it replied, "In the beginning, when you first sought to commune with me, I thought you were the same ilk as King Telinor and his star wraiths. It was only before you came here that I saw something more. There is great power stirring within you, Zolan. It has been many centuries since I've seen a magician awakened by a god. *That* is why I brought you here, for a sorcerer called forth by Calamtu is always an intriguing matter."

"You know my name?" he asked.

"I know many things," was its answer. "You do not realize how open your mind is when using telepathy."

The slits of the feline's eyes narrowed further. "If you wish to escape this realm and receive my aid, you must prove that you know how to harness this power. Perhaps Calamtu knows what significance you hold to the world, but I am not convinced of it myself."

"Is there no other way you can help us?" said Stormbright. "Most times, I would have no problem in passing this 'test' of yours, but my friends and family are dying out there, and we need your power just this once."

The creature snickered, smiling so its fangs were bared like a vampire. "War, death, famine," it mused. "'It's the way the world has always worked. And truly, all things are wiped clean with the inexorable passage of time. No, Zolan. I can only accept a proper demonstration of your skill. Otherwise, I am afraid there is nothing I can do."

The youth remained silent for several moments. "Very well," he said reluctantly. "I will accept this challenge of yours, though I don't know what it entails."

"Excellent," it purred. "Let us begin."

Stormbright saw that the manticore had disappeared, the only trace of it showing as a strange, almost tangible light. He looked up to the throne before him, seeing that a figure was lounging upon it.

He stood there in disbelief. It was General Caerst.

"I see that one of my slaves has returned to grovel," she mocked. "First I would have you punished for insubordination. Perhaps I shall kill your father before slitting your brother's throat?" She stood, drawing her rapier. "*That* will teach you to defy me."

"But you cannot be-" he stammered, "You cannot be *her*! You're just an illusion created by Oubal—a phantom made to test me."

"Slave—you disappoint me," the Falconer spoke humorously. "If I weren't real, then surely I couldn't harm you. But rest assured that you were never safe from me. I'm always watching, always eager to bring the traitor to heel!"

She sprang forward with a frightening speed, exceptionally so for one fully armored save for a helmet. The tip of her rapier shot forward, and Stormbright was quick enough to unsheath his own sword, sparks flying as he parried and stepped to one side.

He moved to riposte, although his opponent was already stepping backward, the mark of the duelist showing itself clearly within her stance. She thrust forward once again, and again the magician was saved by the skills he had learned from Trilgar.

So they partook in a dance of death as one struck while the other parried, reverting the direction of attack, only for the next blow to be dodged and the cycle begin anew. They fought like the swirling vortex of violet and crimson high over them. Always circling, always intermingling, yet not one side gave to the other.

On and on they fought, until Stormbright felt his strength beginning to waver. He was certain that his opponent would deliver the *coup de grace*, and there would be little he could do once it came.

His fears and suspicions were soon proven correct, for the woman-general took a lightning-quick step forward. The length of her blade grazed his side, yet the magician was otherwise unharmed, as he had barely strafed a lethal blow.

He struck at her wrist, causing the weapon to fly a good distance away. It collided with the amber substance on which they stood, the blade ringing as if it had been smitten against solid stone.

The look she gave was no less daunting, as Stormbright's blade was brought to her throat. "Well done," she said. "But now it's time to finish what you started. Take my life, and you shall have proven that you are indeed my better." She smirked. With a slow, seductive movement, she undid her braid, allowing the golden tresses of hair to fall behind her shoulders.

Warily Stormbright held his stance, not moving one way or the other. He hadn't realized it until now, but her slim, curvaceous form swayed with sensual allurement. She unfastened her cuirass, allowing it to clatter along her feet and reveal her naked breasts.

General Caerst's eyes burned with lustful intensity as she strode forward, not unlike a harlot.

"Or perhaps you would like to take *something else* of mine," she purred, her hands caressing the young sorcerer's features. She brought him closer, taking one of his hands and squeezing it over her bosom. The sensation was electrifying. Her grip was firm, painful, and she moaned in response. "I will not freely give you my body, but that doesn't matter." Her voice lowered to a whisper as it registered within one ear. "You will first have to drive me to submission. I shan't go easily, but I do not doubt you are quite capable of overpowering me.

"Come now, Zolan. You've got the strength in you, and you have the magic of gods at your disposal! Take what is yours, and damn all the consequences! It is not my choice, nor those who stand against you. You are a sorcerer, and it's unto *your* whims that the world should yield."

For a moment, Stormbright stood still, unmoving as the phantom he faced continued its untoward advances, desperately trying to stoke the flames of his basest of humanly wonts.

The youth did not yield.

"You killed the people I love," he spoke. "Your debauchery ends here."

He raised his blade, and before the Falconer could even react, he slashed across her neck…

Her head failed to meet the ground. It was as if a bubble of light had been burst where there should have been a body. The formation of bright, shimmering substance nearly dissipated before it reshaped itself, reforming some distance away into a feline form.

"Most interesting," said Oubal. It seemed to purr with delight as Stormbright sheathed his blade. "Even when I tried provoking your sense of lust and want for power, you remained steadfast. It's surprising that a boy your age should wield these powers with such discipline."

"Well, I have to admit it was a little tempting," he said, catching his breath.

"But you passed. And admirably so, I might add." The creature appeared to smile. "For that, I shall grant you my aid."

The manticore dimmed against the light surrounding it. All Stormbright could see was a faint silhouette reshaping itself, thinning and elongating in a form that was curved and pointed on either end. Its shape was that of an "S."

The Oubal Staff clattered to the ground beside the throne. The magician, wearied from all he had experienced in a short span of time, motioned himself closer to the item, picking it up with both hands. He could feel the spirit of Oubal entwining with his, bringing him power and focus which served to hone his abilities.

He smiled—he would need that power in order to stave off Alcaron's onslaught. Not to mention the real General Caerst.

In a strange sense, it was as if the staff was guiding him subconsciously, for he seated himself atop the blackened throne. He felt a strange warmth spreading throughout his spine, then his limbs and other faculties, as Stormbright's vision began to blur.

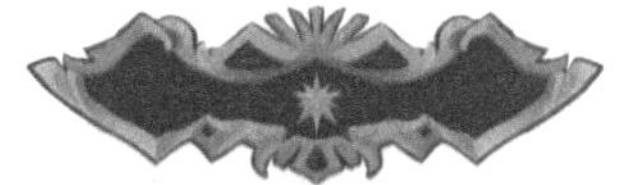

XII

The Quiet Before Dawn

The palace chamber lay silent as the councilmen hung their heads in dismay.

Several nights passed within those decrepit walls, the conversations becoming more heated and intense. Little progress was made in forming an effective strategy against Alcaron, as they were reminded of their enemy's resources, and how theirs, by contrast, were rapidly depleting.

Now all but the wealthiest were on the brink of starvation.

In the beginning, sixteen councilmen sat around the oval table. Queen Kitala declined each motion to surrender to General Caerst, for she knew well what the Ilgrathians were capable of in terms of 'mercy.' Those who dissented fled the boundaries of the city, so that they at least would not be taken prisoner by the enemy.

Others deemed it necessary to swear allegiance to the other side, and with it came one attempt, then a second, against Kitala's life.

In this matter, Shariz'lan proved an effective deterrent, as her astromantic visions showed them who would strike and at what time. Steel was tasked with planning ahead and intercepting the attempts, not to mention delivering the final execution. The relationship between him and Kitala had developed in no small part since their return; she entrusted him fully with her life, even in spite of what her people said in protest.

Soon thereafter, he and Shariz'lan were chosen to replace the seats left absent, along with giving protection should any more plots reveal themselves.

The prospects of formulating a plan continued, but there was little the young thief could do when compared to the others. In truth, he found the whole game of politics to be rather boring. At least there was King Telinor at his side, who though having no discernable face, seemed to echo his sentiments. Often he found himself studying the star wraith's incorporeal body, if for no other reason than to pass the time.

Even so, Steel knew that he would be manning the ground defenses along Miracor's wall. King Telinor and his star wraiths, by contrast, would be combating any assailants from above.

There remained several holes in their plan, and those present knew it well. It was evident that the thief would have to contend with the Ilgrathians' siege engines forged of moonsteel, not to mention thousands of armored soldiers who would be hammering their position. It was only a matter of time before their defenses would crumble.

They would have to find a means of counterattack. Otherwise, there would be no hope for survival. No more Islirians to resist…

Steel pondered this as the council doors were flung wide open. There, supported by Ya'utet, was none other than Stormbright. What was more, all evidence of the sorcerer's wound had disappeared, save for a slight limp to his gait.

"Zolan!" He rose from where he sat, dashing over and wrapping his younger sibling in a warm, tight embrace.

A moment passed before Stormbright pushed himself away. "I never thought you were the caring type," he said.

"Nonsense! We all thought you were dead. How is it you're standing? Surely, your body could not have healed so quickly…"

The youth shook his head, smiling. "Perhaps I would have been under different circumstances. It was the Oubal Staff that saved me. The spirit inside has decided to help us, brother."

"The Oubal Staff?" murmured the sibyl, stepping forward along with Kitala. "But the artifact was taken by myself. I even stored it for safekeeping…"

Stormbright held aloft the black metal stave. The strange artifact glowed with a soft violet light, causing a host of ghostly shadows to flitter among the chamber.

"When I awakened, I saw that the Oubal Staff was lying there at my side. It healed my wounds, although I can hardly believe it, myself…"

He recounted the details of his journey, along with being tested at the manticore's bidding. King Telinor moved closer as the youth continued, the specter showing what might have been an expression of wonder.

"Even I wasn't aware the Oubal Staff could wield such magic. You are fortunate that this spirit has decided to help you. The art of magic healing is rarely seen in Zirvonia, save for the most powerful of creatures."

Stormbright looked toward his friends. "It seems I've interrupted at a crucial time," he said. "If I can help with what you're planning, then I will do it. I hope to deal with the sciomancer once and for all. Now that I have the Oubal Staff at my side, I aim to turn his demons against him and end this siege."

"Perfect! I couldn't have asked for a better plan, myself." Steel grinned.

The star wraith shimmered as he spoke, "You must be sure to dispatch with the sciomancer first. If you were to try and seize control of the demons beforehand, the results could be disastrous. Kitala has informed me of the demonic frenzy from before, as well as how both sides were devastated as a result. The outcome here could be similar should you fail." His voice became more grave. "As for the moment, they are under *his* command. That includes summoning and dismissing them at will. It is probably wise that you should strike when Dimorn's legions are some distance away, then call on the staff once the deed is done."

"And what about you, brother? Isn't stealth normally your forté?"

"I'm needed here. Normally I would accompany you, but I'm expecting that bronze bitch to be at the front line of this assault. She's just as dangerous as Dimorn, possibly more so after her defeat. Besides, I've got a score to settle."

"Attacking from two different angles, I see? Very well," he nodded. "If that is the case, then I will require use of the *Heavens Barge*. It's already proven to be a stealthy and inconspicuous ship, and I get the feeling it will help us here."

"I hold no objections to it, myself," smiled Queen Kitala, moving herself closer to the two. "It's good to see you well, Stormbright."

His expression softened. He hadn't been aware of it until now, but there was a confidence in their words—a hope that things would get better.

It filled him with purpose.

"Come, little brother. There's still much for us to do, and little time." Steel held out his hand. "Let us see this through to the end—together!"

Stormbright looked up to his brother, towards his friends and those who had cared for them these last several weeks. There was a part of him that wanted to weep with joy, though he suppressed the urge with no small effort.

"Right. Together then!"

Their hands clasped in unison. Both knew that the road ahead wouldn't be an easy one. Regardless, they would face it together as one.

Darkness pervaded the tent's interior. A small flame wavered dimly at its center, casting a faint orange light as its fingers caressed the metallic bowl above.

It was during times like these that General Caerst reflected on her purpose, prostrating herself before the symbol of her goddess. The idol of Ilgrathié peered overhead, acknowledging the container of boiling water a short distance away.

The Falconer knew well what this holy water represented: pain, hardship, loss… all necessary steps on the road to enlightenment. Little did the lesser races know that this was the one true way to achieving a better world. Only pain and suffering could make one stronger, and the ones who survived would celebrate in unending pleasures, serving those who were even mightier…

The thought excited her to no end. Her plump breasts brushed the canvas floor and soft pillows, baring each curve of her naked body, as it was illustriously displayed in supplication to the idol. It was natural that pain should be coupled with pleasure during such a rite. And, as if in full acknowledgement of this practice, the two slaves who stood at either side of the tent rigidly held their posture. They were both girls, and having seen little more than fifteen winters, they were deathly afraid of what this Falconer was capable of.

General Caerst rose slowly to her knees. As was customary for such prayers, she presented herself in as alluring a manner as possible to her goddess. Her smooth legs became entangled with her pillows. Her back arched so that her buttocks were more clearly defined. The heat and steam brought about a thin layer of perspiration, the area between her thighs warming with restless anticipation.

Her body shivered as she gave a low, passionate moan…

No—not yet. Not until the battle was done.

Now was the time for foreplay.

Her voice mingled with the supreme, acquiescent silence of her chambers, as she caressed the figure of her goddess. She rested her head against a stony thigh while muttering a low prayer. To her chagrin, the words echoed in her ears like thunder—an insult, as if by divine providence, of what she had seen.

Though the fault of the massacre lay with the sciomancer, she was still the one who had entrusted him with controlling the demons. She had unleashed horrific death on her own side, despite her good intentions.

That little stunt had cost her hundreds of lives.

 *"The thought excited her to no end."* 

The throng of star wraiths, along with her companion's fiendish subordinates, had forced even the bravest of her men to retreat with full speed. She remembered the crushing sense of defeat she had felt that day, along with glimpsing something else along the horizon.

It was lightning, wielded by a boy whom she barely recognized as one of her own. If it weren't for their newfound cause to dispatch with the traitorous magician, then she would have slain Dimorn by now.

The thought of having a sorcerer at the Islirians' disposal stoked the fires of her rage. She had given the sciomancer his one final chance at salvation; either he would find and dispatch with this "Stormbright," or he would suffer a far worse, more exquisitely painful fate at her own hand.

In the meantime, their correspondence with the city's turncoats had yielded its results: It was reported that Queen Kitala ventured with Steel and Stormbright, and that she was heading deeper into star wraith territory aboard a small flying vessel; the goal of which amounted to little more than pursuing a legend. If it weren't for the dangerous, ghastly specters, along with the distance the trio had covered, then surely she would have intercepted them.

Dimorn proposed a less costly tactic: "Instead of pursuing them," he said, "it would be better if we set up an ambush. Then, once they return, they will find that they are right where we want them."

Despite her own grievances, the plan was remarkably sound. An ambush was set, and it was a few days before the sciomancer had made his return, reporting that the brother who wielded the lightning was slain. He would have killed the others had his concentration not been exhausted. Not only that, but the wound he sustained exacerbated the process.

The sciomancer's strength and concentration were fast waning. The thief's arrow had struck him in a vital area, and even Alcaron's specially-trained healers could only do so much to keep him alive and standing.

It was now up to General Caerst to use her cunning, as well as the special siege engines she had brought in her absence.

Come either eventuality, Alcaron's victory was assured.

She reached out to the steaming basin at her side, while the flaps of the tent parted. She heard the voice of the Almari commander, who spoke with a slight quaver to his voice, as he reported his squadron's status.

The uneasiness was made all the more apparent to her trained senses, as men were indeed predictable creatures.

"And why is it you're reporting at this moment?" she murmured.

The Almari Commander spoke: "My subordinates have spotted a cosmic veil encompassing the city. Without a doubt, it is those star wraiths who make this area their haunt. They seem to be swarming in greater numbers than I've ever seen."

"Why should this concern me now?" General Caerst inquired further, her hands clasping the iron of the bowl. There was a distinct hissing sound as flesh made contact. Yet there was no hint of pain, as she raised the container high over her head. "It is just a sign that the Islirians are dying as we speak. The less there are of them, the more star wraiths who rise as a result."

"Not if what your sorcerer claims is true," said the Ilgrathian. "If the star wraiths have chosen to ally with their enemies, this could bring ill omens for us all."

"If that were true, then we should have received a message from our spies within the city."

"And what *have* you received from them?"

"Nothing," she replied. "That is what concerns me."

She upturned the bowl, allowing the scalding water to pour over her supple frame, her bronze skin flushing red with the heat. To anyone who wasn't a chosen Falconer, the experience would have proven debilitating… perhaps even fatal. Yet for General Caerst, the pain tingled along her nerve senses, bringing her ecstatic pleasure, as her imperfections were burned away.

She could sense the commander's glare in her direction. With a wave of her hand, the two mistresses moved from their standing places, each with newly-made attire suited to fit her alluring figure.

The Falconer sighed. "Very well—if you are so concerned about these star wraiths, then I will rouse Dimorn and have him stand close by, ready to summon his demons should anything unexpected occur. I believe I've just the potion to boost his vitality. It won't last forever, but it should help to prevent our previous incident."

"As you command," nodded the Almari Commander, turning to leave. "Thank you, General."

With that, the Falconer was alone.

General Caerst sighed as she spared a glance to one of her servants. She saw the uneasiness creep into the girl's eyes as she was being dressed.

She heightened her servant's discomfiture—honing it to a fine, insidious point—as a finger passed over the thin fabric of the girl's gown, briefly caressing her nipple.

The youth's eyes flared in hatred. General Caerst could sense her fear. Her displeasure. Her desire to slay her master…

She relished it all.

"Dear slave," she purred, "bring me my dagger."

A silent moment passed before the young woman obeyed. There was a second as if she pondered whether now would be the best time to strike. Reluctantly, she chose against it…

The Falconer felt along the edge of her blade, admiring the cold moonsteel that had been folded several times over in service to their cause. Her tongue slid along its surface, her eyes closing as it reached past the sharpened tip. She smiled, bringing it down before driving it forward. A gurgle was made in reply, as the one slave fell supine, the dagger driven between her ribs.

The slave's breathing stopped… She was dead.

"You should have killed me when you had the chance."

Despite seeing the death of her friend, the remaining slave did not falter as she fitted the Falconer with a helm and cuirass of moonsteel, both embossed with delicate brass patterns. The Rite of Supplication was complete—pain and pleasure—as the frail, shapely creature took on heroic proportions. No longer was she the wretch who prayed and slew in the dark. She was General Caerst— the hero who would deliver her people unto victory.

She stood atop the rocky escarpment outside their war camp. Pride swelled in her bosom, her Ilgrathian bloodlust overcoming her other emotions.

"To arms, my Falcons!" Her words rang above the vast and innumerable host of armored figures. An issuance of footsteps quickened in tempo as ranks were deftly formed. Shields and hauberks of bronze and moonsteel were donned as voices were silenced, campfires doused in the blink of an eye. Before a minute had passed, the formation was complete.

Silence reigned supreme among the armies of Alcaron.

A path was formed among their number, and General Caerst began her march among the barren, blackened waste. The air was dry; it tasted of ashes that clung to her armor. The stench was one of death—sickly sweet—or was that just her feverish imagination? Each footstep rang like the tolling of a bell, her own voice magnified a hundred-fold by the surrounding emptiness as she addressed her soldiers in kind.

"Fellow brothers, I arrive before you today without ceremony, for I must enlist your skill and resolve before we advance. Once more I ask that you risk your lives for Ilgrathié, so that we might succeed where our mercenaries have failed. By daybreak, we shall number the city of Miracor among our own, and we will have gained a whole host of slaves for our enjoyment!

"I say to you: will you not join me in this conquest? Shall you cower on this pivotal day of our history—or will you fight?"

"We will fight!!" her soldiers shouted their battle cries, thumping their spears along the blasted ground.

She continued: "Take heed, my men! It's a grave error to underestimate our enemies, especially ones who were once so mighty that their legacy stands before us. Worry not, for their knowledge shall soon be ours. They will bow down before our goddess, and those who fight shall perish before our holy crusade!

"This fallen race shall not be permitted to continue their treachery! Their crimes are too great! Their treachery too profound! So I ask that you join me in this fight, that we may venture forth and cleanse this world of another evil!"

The cries and shouts erupted once more, this time even louder than it was previously. It was clear that her army's morale was coming to a peak. She marched forth from whence she stood, the armies of Alcaron quick to follow. Only Dimorn and the Almari hadn't joined them in their pursuit.

Following several long minutes of silence, save for the rattling of metal and the howling wastes, they arrived at the threshold of that ruined city. All was going well so far, she surmised. Now came the easy part.

"Enemies of Ilgrathié, I would have your ear for a moment." Her words echoed over the heads of her armored soldiers. This time the wasteland no longer bolstered her voice. It seemed a small and frail thing; yet even so, it held no lesser sway over the crowd.

At first there was no answer. For a time it appeared all would remain silent, and that Miracor was just an abandoned citadel, empty and ripe for plundering. General Caerst did not waver in her stance, before a solitary figure craned its head over the distant rampart.

"And what might this general have to say?" The Islirian spoke solemnly, his accent indicating that he was quite young for a native of Miracor.

General Caerst glared above her. "My men and I have arrived in the name of conquest. We would give you this one chance to surrender. Submit yourselves now, and we will show you mercy."

"My companions and I have already considered your offer," said the Islirian. "We have decided to decline. Simply put, if you hope to take our city from us, then you will have to pry it from our cold, dead fingers."

The Falconer lowered her head, hiding the grin which spread across her lips. "It seems that war is our only recourse, then. Remember this moment well, dearest messenger, as it shall mark the downfall of you and your brethren."

She took a step back, turning to face her men who looked at her expectantly. Clearly they were ready for the battle to commence.

So was she.

"Then if our enemies will not surrender unto the Falcon," she said, raising her voice, "they shall feel our rending talons!"

The armies of Alcaron rang in unison with a mighty war cry. To General Caerst, they appeared like statuesque figures, animated for the sole purpose of her unwavering, uncompromising command. She looked forward to the city walls, feeling the rallying spirits of her soldiers intermingling with her own heated bloodlust.

It was all or nothing. Raising her rapier in a defiant stance, her voice carried over the entirety of the battlefield.

"Charge, my men!" she cried. "Do not stop until every Islirian is slain, every woman raped and child enslaved! For our goddess, for your honor, do not stop until it is done!!"

The first arrow was loosed, the armored boots of the Ilgrathians moving in perfect sync.

So began the battle for Miracor.

XIII

The Battle of Miracor

Steel gazed over the city wall while Ya'utet returned. As the thief had anticipated, the Islirian's expression was a melancholic one.

"Sounds like it's war, then?" His words were less inquiry and more assertion.

The warrior nodded. "Alcaron's armies are moving with incredible speed," he said. "It's as if their goddess is leading them herself."

"Knowing our luck, that may well be the case."

Queen Kitala stood at his side, whetting her blade as the tempest of voices rang out from underneath. At her side was a shortbow and a quiver of two-dozen arrows.

He moved himself beside her. "I'm surprised you're joining me on the wall. Risking your life with us, that is."

She grimaced. "It's better than simply languishing in some palace and waiting for the end. Besides, all my lieutenants know their orders, and they would carry them out even if I were to perish in battle."

Steel nodded, smiling with a profound sense of admiration. "How well do you handle a bow?" he asked.

"Well enough, though my marksmanship isn't as good as yours."

From below, they could hear their enemies' cries growing to an almost deafening volume. Steel's only wish was that his brother would be quick with executing their plan. Otherwise, it seemed they would be crushed by the vast numbers of soldiers…

He pushed the fear out of his mind as he walked towards the edge of the battlements. Rows and rows of archers ran along either side, as well as soldiers who piled up large rocks to pelt their enemies from above. It seemed there were hundreds of defenders standing at their position, though Steel knew deep down it wouldn't be enough.

Even from this distance, he could overhear General Caerst's rallying speech, those thunderous shouts instructing her men to slay and burn and take what was theirs. The Ilgrathians stood before the city in the nameless thousands, spears and pikes pounding the ground in rhythm. Dozens of armored bodies lingered close to the wall. Some distance away, thin ranks of archers withdrew their weapons and waited, along with massive siege engines forged of shimmering moonsteel.

Damn that bitch! Never before had he known a person to wield such enthusiasm, especially one who wished them all dead.

A final series of shouts erupted forth… then the enemy began its charge for the gates. "Hold fast, men!" shouted Ya'utet, as he, Steel, and Queen Kitala took cover, ducking behind the stone slats, narrowly avoiding a volley of arrows which darkened the sky over them.

The sounds of the wounded and flint scraping on stone met Steel's ears. They recovered their positions. "Loose!" he yelled, releasing an arrow himself.

Their bowstrings sang in unison. The rain of projectiles sped forth, sinking into the undulating mass of Ilgrathian soldiers. The armor of their enemies was strong, yet their aim was no less true. Arrows sank between joints, striking underneath helmets, and a surprising number of soldiers fell before them.

Another hail of missiles sprang towards their position. Only this time, Ya'utet was struck in the neck by one he hadn't seen.

The Islirian collapsed to the ground, gurgling and bleeding for several seconds before his movements slowed and stopped.

There came no time for remorse as the battle raged onward. The sounds of metal and groaning wood could be heard out in the distance, as Steel and Kitala saw that the siege engines were coming closer, firing upon the walls. The first stone catapulted well over them, landing in a desolate area along the city behind. They were not so lucky with the second shot, as a ballista bolt landed squarely below whence they stood, bringing a violent tremor from underneath their feet.

Steel's hopes fell further, as once again he spotted the hundreds of scaly wings emerging from the distant horizon. They had come earlier than he expected. The demonic host roared across the skies, their tattered wings not compromising their speed in the slightest.

"Now!" he shouted.

Looking over his shoulder, he saw the Star Towers thundering into life; their beams glanced over the plain with deadly precision; siege engines, winged demons, and Ilgrathian soldiers were caught in its voluminous rays. Despite their exceptional make and tolerance to heat, many of the war machines were rendered inert, cables and gears snapping under the suffocating heat of it all. Hundreds of scaly demons careened out of the skies with each blast, collapsing in a heap of roaring flames.

The three parties made their inexorable advance, as their combined forces outnumbered the defenders five-to-one.

Suddenly, King Telinor and his army of star wraiths sprang into action. The specters ascended with startling speed, appearing to the young thief as one great, borderless tear in the fabric of reality, studded by the occasional cluster of stars in their cosmic veil. Their forms shimmered while rising high over both armies—even the Islirians' magic towers—before colliding with the mass of demons.

The effect was immediate and terrible. Wraith and hellspawn clashed without restraint, their shrieks and howls accentuating the despair that permeated the battlefield.

At that moment, the entire world—both above and below— seemed to reshape itself into a sea of warring bodies. The stench of dirt and burning corpses filled the nostrils of those who fought and slew. The only distinction among the chaos were the vibrant hues of light reflecting off metal armor, coupled with flowing blood.

Steel loosed arrow after arrow until he recognized that *something else* was heading in their direction.

They were the enemy's forces of Almari—the elite rukh riders who brandished skewer and javelin in the name of bloodshed.

A frightening gust of wind was produced as the Almari sped past the wall's defenders. Steel, Kitala, and several others turned— refocusing their aim—firing at the riders who assaulted the flame- lancing spires.

More and more of the defenders joined in that endeavor, as they knew well that if Miracor's towers should fall, they were doomed.

The young thief poured every ounce of energy he had into his arms and fingers, releasing arrow after arrow in rapid succession. Suddenly, he heard a splintering sound as javelins were hurled against the orbs. There came another horrific *crack*, then another.

Following the rain of attacks from above, Miracor's towers were destroyed, each one followed up by a fiery blue explosion.

Even so, Steel didn't cease as his rage took full hold. The fury of his heart became transfixed with his weapon, his aim focused on the Almari's leader.

He fired a single shot, wounding the commander's rukh in a vital area. Both mount and rider fell among the vast streets below. Several more bodies followed, as the ranks of Almari were thinning because of the Islirian archers.

Those who survived retreated as best they could, back to where the fighting wasn't as intense.

"Come back and fight me, you cowards!" shouted Steel, his anger blazing from every fiber of his being, blotting out any sense of reason or mercy. "If you ever return, know that my bow and dagger are trained at your hearts! I will not hesitate to end your pathetic lives!! Do you hear me?!"

His arrows didn't stop, even though his allies redirected their attacks below.

A hand moved over his arm, lowering his aim before he could continue.

It was Kitala.

Steel returned to his senses, allowing his rage to subside. It didn't disappear so much as it crept into some dark corner of his psyche, locking itself away for another time.

He sighed as he allowed her to guide him behind the wall, crouching and catching his breath while the fighting had slowed. He found it was a moment he sorely needed.

"It seems our defenses are ready to crumble," he said, looking into the depths of her eyes. "I'm afraid if my brother doesn't complete his mission, we'll all be dead before the hour is past."

"Don't worry yourself," replied Kitala, placing her hand along his arm. "Stormbright will come through for us. Of that I have no doubt. We must keep together, face General Caerst and end her life once and for all. Right now, she is well-armored and protected. Even your best shot could not kill her from this distance. We must wait for the proper time to strike if we hope to survive."

Steel nodded. "You're right—though frankly, I don't expect either of us to live through this." His hand brushed lightly along her face, his mood one of passion. "If I should die here, then I will gladly do so if it means that you and my brother can live free from tyrants."

She smiled, and their lips met as they embraced each other.

Suddenly, there came the shouts of their enemy, along with the groaning of the siege engines. Steel and Kitala rose from their position, returning to the heated chaos of battle. The city walls gave another violent shudder, and they were once again in a fight for their lives.

The cries came to Stormbright's attention as he piloted the *Heavens Barge*, adjusting its flight so it took on a northerly course. The city of Miracor stood behind him—a scene of utter pandemonium.

He could not look back on it now. His quest demanded his full attention.

The youth felt the Oubal Staff over his shoulder—the stave reaching into his mind and enhancing his focus—guiding him forward to his objective. He turned the crank closest to him, and the ship lowered its altitude. The levitation orb pulsed in a heartbeat rhythm, even though it was a trifle slower than it had been before.

The young sorcerer was nearly obscured by the close distance he held to the ground. Thankfully, no demons or Almari flew close to him—otherwise he would have surely been spotted.

Stormbright knew that he was coming closer to the Ilgrathian's war camp. He landed and disembarked at the foot of a large escarpment, the top of which marked the edge of the settlement. He was vaguely familiar with the area, and from above, he could hear the recognizable screeches of the Almari's rukhs.

It was strange to think that so few of the elite soldiers had flown after his departure. Perhaps the tide of battle was turning?

Stormbright shook off the thought, studying the rocky path before him. Although there was little space to walk along, a few piles of boulders allowed an easy enough ascent.

That accounted for nearly half the way up, he mused. The rest would be far more difficult.

Regardless, the young sorcerer began his climb without hesitation. The mere notion of that would have shocked the same boy from two years ago. That person would have faltered and questioned his ability, before giving up entirely.

However, he was Zolan no longer. He and his brother had died in their own way at the hands of the Ilgrathians. They were broken by those stinging whips, reshaped by the sounds of innocents being tortured, mutilated, and defiled.

It was enough to test their own desire to live. But they survived. What remained was no longer the two brothers of their youth. Zolan was Stormbright—his brother, Steel—and they would save the people of their newfound home, no matter the cost.

He carried on in his climb, not once failing to check the sturdiness of his path before advancing.

It wasn't long before he reached the halfway point. As expected, the ledge remained narrow and thin, with there being no obvious way forward save for climbing. He was forced to use his hands and feet, much like he had before with the amber tree, as he grabbed at outcroppings and reliefs wherever available.

A few moments later, he was close to the top. Leaning against the cliff-face, Stormbright shot another glance towards the lofty summit. The strange sense of vertigo was nearly too much as he felt his sense of balance wavering, his body tilting backwards into the abyss…

He caught himself at the last second. Stormbright steadied himself, estimating that he was well over three-quarters of the way there. Just a little farther, he told himself.

Resuming his advance and moving a little ways short of the precipice, he could hear the chatter of two voices above him.

He halted all movements, his muscles straining to keep perfectly still while the Ilgrathians spoke in turn.

"You cannot keep me here," said one soldier. "My sword is required if we're to win this battle." Judging by its timbre, Stormbright guessed the boy was quite young; not much older than himself, in all likelihood.

"Don't be foolish, boy," retorted the other, one who sounded much older and more experienced. "Our sciomancer is wounded in our camp, and we are short on healers as is. We must remain here and tend to him while he weaves his magicks. Think about our role and how important we are—we are the last remaining defenders between our sorcerer and some assassin."

"Pah! It is not the same. Ilgrathié rewards only the brave, and I won't sit idly by while the chance for glory is at our doorstep. I crave battle, father! You will not hold me from this path."

A moment of silence, then, "If that is your wish, then I shan't deprive you of it… Come—let us rejoin the others." The man let out a sigh as they paced away from the cliff-side, leaving Stormbright alone.

Without hesitation, he pulled himself over the cliff's edge. His breath steadied as he peered over the boulder which served as cover. Before him lay a clearing, bereft of life it seemed, save for a stable which housed the monstrous warbirds. Luckily, the rukhs hadn't noticed him yet…

Stormbright smiled. Even though he wasn't an expert in stealth like his brother, he remained hidden thus far.

Seeing no more signs of the soldiers, the boy stole silently as he could from cover-to-cover, taking the utmost care that he stay hidden. He peeked into one tent, then another, in the hopes of finding Dimorn.

Alas, there was no luck so far. That left the other half of the camp to investigate. Surely, one of them had to be the sciomancer's shelter…

Soon enough, the youth heard the distinct murmuring of voices. They were coming closer to his position. He dove into one of the tents closest to him—one he hadn't yet explored.

He saw that an Ilgrathian was facing in his direction. There was a momentary silence as the two stood dumbfounded, then reacted.

The soldier made to shout and draw his sword, but Stormbright's blade was slightly faster.

The man slumped to the ground as his diaphragm was pierced by the weapon, his breath escaping in a low wheeze, not a syllable uttered.

Stormbright cursed under his breath, retrieving his weapon from the corpse. He couldn't understand how Steel fought like this so often—killing unexpectedly from the shadows.

He didn't have time to think of it any longer. The sorcerer let his feelings pass as he moved himself closer to the flaps of the tent. Though he couldn't see anything directly from where he crouched, the sound of footsteps was no less recognizable to his ears. There must have been four of them at least—a number he could scarcely deal with without resorting to his use of magic. Once the first lightning bolt was hurled, he knew there would be no going back.

"Where's my son?" asked one of the soldiers, whose voice Stormbright recognized from earlier. "I thought he was here a moment ago. He was supposed to join us at the edge of camp before we ventured closer to the siege." The Ilgrathian shouted, "Jalkar, where are you?"

"He is likely joining the battle as we speak," Dimorn chuckled. "In candor, Paldar, you should have seen that he was trained more thoroughly before bringing him here. The boy is too young. He has too fiery a temper for his own good."

"Perhaps so, sir," said the Ilgrathian. "I thought this war would put some hairs on the boy's chest. You know we aren't truly tested until entering the throes of battle. I figured it would be best to expose him to it sooner rather than later."

"And rest assured, he *will* be tested. You put too much faith in his eagerness, and not enough in discipline. Now look where it has got him. The boy is reckless, Paldar…"

Stormbright hesitated as the outside conversation continued. His goal was a short distance away. Yet there was the obstacle of Paldar and the remaining guards, not to mention the resistance the sciomancer himself would bring.

It was all or nothing, he told himself. As if in a kindly gesture, he could feel his fears being assuaged by the Oubal Staff. That gave him some form of confidence. He thanked it in kind, even though he didn't say a word aloud.

He also thanked Calamtu, the one who had awakened his powers in the first place.

Taking a slow breath, Stormbright burst out of the darkness and into the open, the lightning coursing along his fingers…

He would not fail this time.

XIV

A Duel of Magicians

The Ilgrathian invaders perished by the hundreds. However, their advance was inevitable as General Caerst rallied them forward, her will dominating over the fields of death.

The Falconer rejoined her companions along the main gates, preparing for the final push. The screams of the dying rose to near-deafening levels about them, and it was all she could do to keep her men in line, barking out orders in rapid sequence. Even if their battering ram hadn't been shielded by close-fitted planks, she would have stayed there all the same—a defiant figure in the face of death.

The invasion was going well—exceedingly so, in fact. She was convinced that victory loomed around the next corner.

That was when an arrow sank into her arm. General Caerst turned her bloodied face above, towards the place where it had originated. She vaguely recognized the young man who stood before her, one who brandished a longbow in his hand, the other poised with another projectile.

Her heartbeat quickened, realizing that this must have been Steel. The man seemed somewhat familiar judging by his appearance, yet she wasn't certain as to where she had seen him before. Regardless, she could feel the hatred radiating in her direction. It was evident that only *she* could have brought such ire from a human…

The thought pleased her exceedingly.

A dozen more soldiers joined alongside her, replacing the dead who had been dispatched by the enemy's arrows. They thundered forward with their ram, causing a terrible rending of wood, as the doors were flung wide, allowing them entrance.

Before the Islirians could retaliate against their invaders, General Caerst and her soldiers were pushing forward, dozens of them filtering in the gates by the minute.

Their armies were flanked on all sides, surrounded by the common peasant turned soldier. Rusted swords and splintered cudgels were borne against them, the inhabitants of Miracor having nothing left to lose.

The Falconer remained unperturbed as she strode forward and the bloodshed began in earnest. She charged, her rapier striking with serpent-like efficiency. The first man she stabbed through the heart, while the next she vigorously beheaded with a swipe of her blade.

She eagerly fought against the full might and aggression of her enemies. Meanwhile, she reveled in the metallic stench of spilt blood, along with the putrid aroma of flesh that was beginning to burn. How wonderful it was, she thought, to experience the chaos of battle! The thrill of it was like liquid fire being pumped through her veins. Every fiber of her being was focused on that grisly task before her—one she embraced with no small amount of pleasure.

Her debauchery was cut short, however, as she felt a second arrow being trained at her heart. She was aware of it through her heightened Falconer senses—another blessing by Ilgrathié. With a swift motion she avoided the projectile, the wooden shaft echoing as it clattered listlessly along the cobbled ground.

"Your timing and aim are impressive," she remarked, "you would be wise in facing me directly."

She turned once more, avoiding the shortsword that swiped at her back. Her rapier shot upward, parrying the blade by a razor's margin, before she moved back several paces.

Her opponent regarded her with a hateful glare.

"And you must be Queen Kitala. I've heard stories of your prowess in battle, but believe me when I say they do you a disservice."

"Enough talking, she-devil!" Kitala hissed between her teeth. "You and your goddess are nothing more than degenerates! I will not stand idly by as you destroy my people!"

Another arrow sang forth from above; the Falconer easily dodged it. Her resolve wasn't diminished in the slightest, as she thrust again with her blade, her eyes flickering here and there in the direction of her hidden assailant.

The reveal was quicker than she had anticipated, as Steel emerged from an overhead balcony. He drew his spear, the anger showing in his eyes. Following her dance of blades with Miracor's Queen, the thief began stabbing repeatedly. Somehow, she managed to stay on her feet, even though she had sustained more wounds than any ordinary person could imagine.

The whirlwind of thrusts and parries continued. General Caerst grimaced. She wouldn't be able to keep this up if she didn't do something quickly. Now parrying both their attacks, she closed distance and went on the offensive. Steel was caught off-guard himself, as he fell backward from a slash along his chest. Likewise,

Kitala was struck along her wrist, the blade careening several cubits away from her position.

The Queen looked towards the Falconer as an opening presented itself. It was an expression of fear. General Caerst had won!

"Kitala!" Steel tried moving back to his feet, but it was already too late. His enemy didn't hesitate before moving and impaling with her blade. The weapon rang true as it sank into the woman's chest, piercing her heart.

With a searing, monumental effort, he regained his composure, tears welling up in his eyes as he brandished his spear and charged forward. The thought of Kitala's death dominated his mind. He shouted in thunderous fury, and his attacks were quick and relentless as he sought to end his mortal enemy.

"You heathen bitch! Bloodsucking harlot! I'll tear out your heart and leave it for the crows! I'll kill you a thousand times over until there's nothing left to destroy!!"

A smirk crossed her features as she deflected the weapon in turn, this time slashing along his arm. The cut was deep, yet Steel shook it off as if it were a minor wound.

Her retaliation was immediate, as she stepped to one side, driving her weapon forward as she had done with Kitala. The thief sidestepped just in the nick of time, the blade narrowly avoiding his ribs.

She would not let him recover. By the time he had regained his stance, she was already upon him. The young thief blocked her rapier with his spear haft, though it was obvious that time was running out.

Making for the final lunge, the Falconer shot forward again with her rapier. She moved in close to where her opponent couldn't parry, straight for the heart.

Her plan partially succeeded. Instead of hitting a vital area like she had planned, Steel twisted so that her rapier only grazed his arm. Dropping his spear, he drew a dirk using his remaining hand.

The blade shot downward, sinking between pauldron and chestplate. General Caerst backed away in a stupor, removing the dagger and tossing it aside while Steel retrieved his weapon. The wound was deep, but not fatal.

"Your attacks mean nothing to me," she remarked. "Ilgrathié protects those who remain devout to her—even in the face of death."

So their dance resumed its deadly tempo. The gathering clouds murmured their implications overhead. Lightning struck with the rapping of metal on wood.

Stormbright fell behind the cover of a nearby tent, as two of the four guards were incinerated by his lightning bolt. Their blackened corpses lurched to the ground at once. One of the surviving sentries lay horribly wounded on his back, the greater part of his body showing a horrific series of burns. The fourth, however, had somehow managed to disappear from the arena entirely. The sorcerer remained on guard as he collected himself, conjuring another ball of lightning out of thin air.

"Impossible!" shouted the sciomancer, who settled along the tent opposite to him. "How? How are you not dead?!"

Stormbright smiled. "My brother and I are more capable than you think," he said.

He emerged from cover, launching the sphere of energy along with several more. The impacts were so explosive that they collided at first with one tent, then another. Within half a minute, nearly everything surrounding the sciomancer was on fire.

He was prepared to hurl another blast towards his target, but before he could do so, he spotted another soldier moving through the flames. The Ilgrathian had hidden himself well amongst the carnage, and so Stormbright was surprised when the man charged to his position. Paldar reared up his blade, swinging wildly at the youth who dared to infiltrate their camp. The man's fair features were masked under a fiery rage, the lights of his eyes showing the unbridled fury that was characteristic of his people.

Stormbright drew his own shortsword, intercepting the attack and bringing it a short distance from his face. His whole body quaked under the effort, as the aches from his wounds were swiftly returning.

He parried the swing, his arms screaming as they were allowed a brief moment's respite. His opponent staggered and fell, his stance thrown wide open. Stormbright didn't hesitate before stabbing forward, the weapon running through the Ilgrathian's heart.

With a choke and sputter of blood, his opponent went still. Instinctively, Stormbright felt a measure of pity for the man. He wished there had been some alternative to fighting father and son—some way he could have spared their lives…

The thought sickened him to his stomach. So much had transpired in a short amount of time. Yet he could not linger further on the matter. His objective was a short distance away from him.

The sciomancer shuddered as the young sorcerer faced him, watching the boy take a wary step forward.

"It's over," said Stormbright. "Surrender now, Dimorn, and we can stop this senseless killing."

The sciomancer burst into laughter. "You really call this killing senseless?" he chortled. "Do you think peace *isn't* what I'm trying to achieve? So long as our peoples remain separate, we will always bear the curse of war on our shoulders. Man will slay his fellow man, and even we Ilgrathians are no better by comparison. What I aim for, Stormbright, is to unite us all, bring the world under a single banner.

"Can you not imagine it? A world where there is no war? No famine or death? It is what we've always strived towards. You couldn't glimpse the bigger picture, dear sorcerer. And now you've decided to stand against us in your folly…" He chuckled again. "Foolish boy."

The sciomancer smiled, fleeing as an arrow whisked towards the youth's position. Stormbright had sensed that something was wrong. He dodged in the nick of time, the missile grazing his arm.

He turned, spotting the one soldier who had been severely burned on both feet, firing one arrow after another in his direction. The effort must have taken an incredible amount of willpower to accomplish, not to mention an inhuman tolerance to pain.

The Ilgrathian didn't falter in his attacks.

Stormbright was forced to take cover along the same tent the sciomancer had lurked behind moments prior.

He saw that Dimorn was heading towards the rukh stables, a short dash from where he crouched. It was a marvel the man could move at all, much less so at such a brisk pace!

Stormbright was quick to follow before a hail of arrows came his way. One sank into his shoulder. He groaned in pain, yet he wouldn't allow himself to falter, as slowing down would spell certain doom.

He could hear more voices coming from behind. It was obvious that a number of Ilgrathians had spotted the flames he had created, coming to investigate how their brothers-in-arms were faring.

His situation was growing worse by the second. Adding to his woes was the fact that Dimorn was mounting one of the rukh beasts. A pair of wings spread aloft as the sciomancer clung to his mount, ascending high over the war camp in a matter of seconds.

Again Stormbright cursed, as the gap between him and his target grew by orders of magnitude. He knew that he would have to make pursuit—otherwise, Miracor would be lost.

He could not accept that reality. He *would* not accept it.

Not a second had passed before he arrived at the stables. He didn't have time to saddle the beast next to him—only open the gates of one rukh, climb up on as it tried snapping at his wounds. Stormbright pulled instinctively at the reins and bridle. The bird reared its head with a jolt, nearly throwing him off entirely. Still, he somehow held his grip, with the beast acceding to his will.

He noticed the guards were coming closer, their ranks forming fast in a stolid line of bodies, as they nocked arrows in preparation. A hail of wooden missiles screamed towards his position; yet they landed just short of their intended target. Perhaps the gods were on his side that day. Maybe it was just good fortune. Regardless of the cause, Stormbright made the best of his time as they readied another volley.

He kicked with his legs like he would have done with a horse. To his surprise and relief, the rukh appeared to respond to his command, bringing its mighty bulk outside the stables. Its wings unfolded, waxing to its full length of ten-cubits, before beating furiously against the air. Great, powerful gusts of wind came from below. Stormbright realized that he was flying, soaring through the air, faster than he could have imagined.

It wasn't a moment too late, either. By that time the arrows had missed him by a razor-thin margin. Their flight grew steeper, as they ascended high over the rolling landscape. The youth surveyed the area, searching for the sciomancer who had eluded him.

It did not take long before he spotted a shadow along the horizon, heading in a straight line towards the creatures that fought over Miracor. Stormbright guessed that Dimorn was seeking refuge with his demonic companions. It made sense, considering they would come to his aid if he were close.

Yet for the moment it seemed that Fate was on Stormbright's side, as the distance between him and the sciomancer was closing fast. Before he knew it, the young sorcerer was only a few paces away from his adversary.

He stretched out one of his hands, the other guiding his feathery companion onward. A streak of lightning illuminated the sky under a blinding haze. Alas, it had missed its intended target, the sciomancer reigning aside his rukh with perfect timing.

Nevertheless, Stormbright was closing in, with both of them coasting alongside each other.

He withdrew his blade, striking with the utmost precision. However, his sword found no resistance as it slashed along thin air. Dimorn had moved his mount away in an instant.

He was clearly being toyed with.

Now resheathing his weapon, summoning what little remained of his energy, Stormbright released another lightning bolt. The stream arced away in a number of directions, before dissipating into nothing.

His powers were of little use at this distance. The sciomancer was too quick atop his rukh…

Once again he tried reining his beast closer, even though that seemed to fatigue him now. He could feel the exhaustion creeping in after so much magic use. He imagined that weaving another spell would probably render him unconscious. That is, without taking the utmost care to concentrate, use every spare bit of energy he had left.

It seemed that Dimorn had other plans in mind. The Ilgrathian and his beast moved upward in a twisting semi-circle, passing over the youth's head with a mighty gust of wind. Stormbright turned, seeing that the sciomancer was out of reach and moving fast in the opposite direction.

What was more, they were no longer alone. Three other Almari riders were fast approaching his position, moving past the Ilgrathian who had fled in a moment's notice. They leaned in close to their mounts, their long skewers and moonsteel cuirasses glimmering as they did so.

Stormbright was then stretched to his very limits as he maneuvered his mount in erratic, zig-zagging patterns to avoid his attackers. However, the Almari were trained to deal with just these kinds of maneuvers. Their movements showed a keen malice, as each action was met in kind with a deft strike of their halberds. Luckily, the youth was quick enough to dodge or parry, but only just.

Still, he found himself moving closer into a trap, one that had been carefully laid out for him.

He knew, also, that his rukh couldn't take much more of this kind of flying. His enemies would be diving in for the inevitable *coup de grace*, and it seemed there would be little he could do in retaliation.

The time came quicker than he had hoped, as one of the Almari broke formation, their weapon outstretched, as it careened full speed towards his position.

The pain screamed through his body as the Ilgrathian flitted past. He had maneuvered his own rukh to the side, thankfully to where the cut wasn't deep. He gasped, panting for breath, as he somehow maintained consciousness.

It was then that he spotted an opening from the pit of despair; the Almari had betted too much on killing him with one swift motion, and now his enemy's former position was clear and unguarded.

The youth didn't hesitate, spurring his mount to even greater levels of exertion. They sped on past the other Almari, escaping the area that was meant to keep him trapped and immobile. He was free from their hold! And a short distance away from those demons was Dimorn.

Chancing another look from behind, he saw that the Almari soldiers were closing in. Two of them met along either side of his rukh. A third nearly touched skewer-point with his back. As they drew inward with their weapons, stabbing downward at his mount, Stormbright pulled sharply upward.

The Ilgrathians' skewers pierced each other. Their beasts howled as they careened downward in turn, unwittingly bringing their masters to an untimely death below.

Now only one of their Almari remained. On the other hand, the sciomancer had reached the two flying armies, a number of strange openings showing themselves among the hundreds of demons warring with the star wraiths. Dimorn's mount didn't slacken, however, as they disappeared into one of the fleshy apertures.

Stormbright immediately followed, he and the Almari behind him vanishing in similar fashion—*within* that writhing mass of bodies!

It didn't take long for Stormbright to lose sight of his target. A warm darkness surrounded him on all sides, one that was complete and all-consuming, even though he was well aware of the demons and star wraiths fighting nearby. Fiendish blood poured down from above, and he was nearly caked in the stuff by the time he passed through a dark, starry veil.

It appeared that he and his rukh were coasting along the stars, in a night sky that was clear and azure. The odd demon emerged here or there, splintering the illusion that he was isolated from the world he knew.

There was an odd tranquility to it all. If he wasn't careful, Stormbright mused, then he might even lose sense of reality in this place.

A moment passed before his senses were again on high-alert. The sight of the Almari shouldn't have surprised him in the least, flying in his direction with a skewer held high…

Yet it did! The warrior shot forth with blinding speed, the edge of his polearm slashing along the youth's shoulder, almost to the bone. Stormbright didn't hesitate as he raised his sword, cutting the Almari's jugular vein with a splash of crimson.

Both Ilgrathian and rukh fell into the cosmic vistas below. That left Dimorn, Stormbright told himself, as he stripped a fragment of cloth from his garments, wrapping it over his wound.

The pain was intense. Despite his weariness, however, the youth's resolve held him together as his senses calmed. In truth, he could only guess where his opponent might be hiding. Dimorn could be anywhere in this place—waiting for the right moment to strike…

His eyes dilated as the solution dawned on him. He would have to make full use of his magic *inner sense*, channel the energy which resided at the core of his being. The same power had allowed him to detect illusions and otherworldly creatures alike. Perhaps it would also help him to locate his enemy—detect the magic trace that would lead him to his foe.

Stormbright held his rukh in place, the creature appearing to flap without rhyme or reason among the formless cosmos. The sorcerer cleared his mind as he went through the necessary meditations. All five of his senses became dulled. It was as if he was peering at the world in a completely different manner, that being through his mind.

The landscape was changing all around him. Suddenly, he realized that he and his mount were surrounded by the amorphous star wraiths, and just farther out were the demons they warred with. That made sense, considering the strange anatomy of the specters. However, he hadn't expected the illusion to be so complete, so befuddling to one's senses…

 *"The warrior shot forth with blinding speed..."* 

He was glad that King Telinor was at his side—otherwise he would have surely been devoured by the countless wraiths.

It was no longer important. Stormbright sensed another presence in that chaos, registering as a distinctive hue to his mind's eye. The figure was a short distance away, and he didn't doubt that it was the sciomancer Dimorn hiding from him.

He motioned his rukh forward, bringing it to a full speed, as he held his bloodied shortsword aloft. It appeared that instead of him flying through some otherworldly space, the bodies of star wraiths were passing him by as individuals, followed by scores of demons distracted by their own little skirmishes.

His focus didn't waver, as he emerged into the same clearing as Dimorn.

The sciomancer turned, his face draining of all its color and vitality. The youth had clearly taken him by surprise. Stormbright swung his blade. Hardly a gasp was made before the man's head parted from his shoulders.

The Ilgrathian's corpse became lost among the flying bodies below. Without a second to lose, Stormbright withdrew the Oubal Staff, focusing his power within its pulsating form. Now was the ultimate test, he mused. If this didn't work, then all of them were as good as dead…

The demons ceased their fight with the star wraiths, just as quickly as it had begun. All semblance of ferocity departed from their horrific features. It seemed they awaited the command of their new master.

"Listen to me now!" he shouted, his voice thundering as if it were Calamtu himself who spoke. "We move as one against Alcaron! Fly at full speed, creatures of the Great Beyond, and make sure that no Islirian or human is harmed! Go and save Miracor!!"

The resounding chorus of shrieks could not have been mistaken, as if the fiends had understood his words perfectly. They soared towards their objective, their bodies flying in perfect unison, as their previous battle was abandoned.

The cloud of star wraiths dispersed, and Stormbright could distinguish King Telinor from among their number. It seemed the specter smiled at him. The sorcerer returned the gesture, looking forward, himself.

Their flight over Miracor's walls was a swift one. So began the slaughter of their enemies as talons and misshapen teeth tore into their prey, the cries of Ilgrathians ringing in a grand symphony of terror.

The bloodshed returned to the ruined streets. Steel and General Caerst did not relent in their duel, though they had sustained their fair share of injuries. The body of Miracor's Queen lay unmoving, not five cubits from where the Falconer stood.

The hordes of demons and star wraiths swarmed around them, cutting off all forms of egress...

All except one.

General Caerst couldn't believe her eyes. In a moment, the battle had turned completely against them.

She felt a presence reaching along her heels. Looking down, she saw that a cosmic cloud was seeping its way along her leg. A silhouette vaguely resembling a hand reached out to her.

She stepped aside, moving away from the shroud of starry matter.

The specter continued to make its advance. It was then that an Islirian silhouette took shape, the shadow of cosmic substance gathering in a form which Steel recognized.

Kitala.

He smiled. Even from beyond death, she had returned to his side—returned to save the people she had vowed to protect. He stepped forward, seeing that Kitala was beginning to sap away at the Ilgrathian's life essence, even from that distance. General Caerst paled as she continued moving backward, her skin starting to wrinkle like tree bark.

The Falconer was also aware of this. If she didn't do something soon, then her life would surely be over…

"This is not the end… Miracor is mine by right! It was chosen for *me!!*"

She didn't have time to react, as Steel moved forward with his spear, stabbing her shoulder.

She cried out in pain. The thief made to retrieve his weapon. As he did so, the polearm was wrenched from his grasp. Steel felt himself tripped over by the Falconer's boot. His head collided with the flagstones, and it wasn't until several minutes later that he regained consciousness.

He braced himself, moving up and looking around, seeing that he was surrounded by allies, as well as the star wraith of his beloved. He gritted his teeth, even as blood trickled down his head, his fist slamming onto the ground whilst his enemy's words echoed in his mind.

This is not the end.

General Caerst had escaped.

XV
The Road Ahead

"You are still planning on leaving us?" Shariz'lan asked.

Without a word Stormbright nodded, his hair waving in the wind as he looked onward, eyes passing over the rolling hills and mountains to the north.

The sibyl gazed warmly at the youth as they stood high atop the city wall. She knew how important it was for the brothers to move forward. They couldn't stand idly by and accept their place in life, especially not after what had happened to them. Not after what happened to Kitala.

Soon they would be taking the fight to Alcaron—someway, somehow.

They had grown so much in just a short span of time. She was loath to see either of them go. If this was Fate's sense of humor, then it was a twisted and malignant one, indeed.

"Are you certain he is still alive? Your father… Kolthan?"

The youth nodded. "I know he's alive. I prefer to think our friend up north will hold true to his promise, keep him safe until we return. If we can find him again, then I believe there is hope for us all."

"Perhaps," said the crone, shrugging her gaunt, bony frame, "but you are also endangering yourselves with this pursuit. You must realize that word will have spread among the Ilgrathians by now. Rest assured that Alcaron *will* be looking for you."

"And General Caerst?" Stormbright added.

"I'm not sure. Normally, after a disaster like this, she would be condemned and executed for her crimes. However, I get the feeling she will escape and pursue you as well."

"Then it's all the more reason for us to leave and search for him. Would you not wish to save your loved ones, even if there was the slimmest chance they were alive?"

The crone sighed, giving him a thoughtful look. "I understand," she said. "It's just sad to see the both of you go. If you ever decide to return, know we will always have a place for you here in Miracor."

Stormbright turned to her, smiling. "It's useless to worry," he said. "But thank you—for everything. Steel and I would love to return someday... though we're not sure when that would be."

"How is your brother, by the way? Last time I saw, he seemed awfully distraught over Kitala. Even though he's trying not to show it."

"Not well. As much as it pains me to say, he will simply have to make do. Both of us know that." He lingered a moment before continuing, "Still, I don't think I've seen him this depressed since we were taken as slaves. Does Kitala remember him, even now as a star wraith?"

The sibyl shook her head. "No. Not even her own guardian," she said.

"That's what I thought."

He saw that his master was choking back tears, silently mourning the woman she had raised. The last heir of Divnarostian nobility. Stormbright had considered the idea of Kitala resuming her reign as her spectral self; however, that would take time and a great amount of discipline. Not to mention the people wouldn't see it so favorably.

First she would have to remember herself, assuming that was a possibility.

Stormbright placed a hand on his master's shoulder, trying as best he could to bring her comfort. She batted the hand away. Despite this, her mood appeared to lighten as he took a step back.

"We will both miss her," he continued. "We'll also remain hopeful that she recovers her memories soon. I have a feeling she will."

"Aye," she nodded. She looked out towards the distant hills beyond, wondering what strange places might be lurking outside the borders of Divnarost. Shariz'lan did not envy her pupil's decision to leave. Even so, there was always a vague wonder she held for the outside world. She could tell that, even though they hadn't mentioned it before, Steel and Stormbright dearly wished to explore Zirvonia.

After a serene moment of quiet, she continued. "Are you certain you want to leave the Oubal Staff with us? It's a great and terrible weapon, Stormbright, and there is always the chance that one of us could misuse it. Knowing our tendencies, it is more than a possibility."

The youth once again nodded. "My decision hasn't changed, Master Shariz'lan. I don't believe anything of the sort will happen—neither by the Islirians or the star wraiths. The staff has a will of its own. Even in my own experience, it *chose* to aid me after determining I was worthy. I do not doubt it would unravel most men and their mad plots in seconds."

"And what about King Telinor and his star wraiths?"

"I believe they'll cling to themselves. For now, at least. Still, if there is any way that your races could maintain peace, then that is probably ideal. There is so much work to be done after these countless years of war. I am not saying it will be easy, mind you, but perhaps there can be a new age of prosperity to come out of this."

The crone pursed her lips. "It is strange that I should be given counsel from one so young. I do not doubt the truth of your words. I shall heed them in the weeks and months to come. You are wise beyond your years, Stormbright, and I believe your brother is lucky to have you."

He chuckled as he replied, "His temper *does* get the better of him, sometimes."

"And your naiveté gets the better of you," she retorted, laughing as well. Stormbright grinned, realizing that she was indeed correct. He and Steel needed each other, just as much as they needed their father.

She continued: "In all sincerity, I envy you. To walk freely on the face of Zirvonia is unlike anything you could imagine. Savor it while you can. I shall pray to Sutana that your journey is a safe one, and that you find Kolthan alive and well."

"We will," he nodded. "Thank you."

Stormbright gathered what remained of his belongings, rejoining his brother along the streets. Steel's look was one of melancholy, though it was obvious he was trying to hide it.

"How is she doing?" asked the young sorcerer.

"Well enough," he replied. "Kitala seems to be alive and well in her new form. King Telinor is also trying to see her memory restored to what it was."

"Good." Stormbright looked at his brother, his blue eyes searching along the other's green. "Do you still need some time here? I understand if you-"

"No. We leave as soon as we can." His voice lowered, just above a whisper. "Kitala would not have wanted me to stay and mourn for her. I will leave and give her time to remember herself. And if she does not, that is also-"

His words were cut off, as the thief felt his brother's embrace. There was a silent moment as words ceased between the two. Overcoming his reluctance, he returned the gesture, allowing tears to flow down his face.

"She *will* remember you, brother. Of that I'm sure. In the end, it's how we push through the pain that makes us stronger."

They remained like this, before Steel pushed his brother away with a fist. "What, are you some philosopher now?" he said in jest.

The younger brother laughed. "You know, I could be…"

"Not really your style. Come on, Zolan. Let's leave while the day is upon us."

Their packs were slung over their shoulders as they made their march towards the front gates. Though the doors were largely in a state of disrepair, much of it had been mended by the Islirians and star wraiths.

A throng of heads were moving about them, and directly present was Shariz'lan, the *de facto* ruler of Miracor, along with King Telinor at her side. Both brothers were shocked at how quickly they were working with each other. Perhaps, in some cases, war *could* unite instead of only destroy.

They were pleased that the notion of peace wasn't as unlikely as it first seemed.

The large doors parted with a groan, and once again the wild winds tugged at their hair, causing their cloaks to flap this way and that. It appeared the desolation outside was beginning to heal, and the war was becoming a vague and distant memory.

Steel and Stormbright each waved their goodbyes, and they were met with a chorus of cheers in return. After what seemed like several minutes of fond farewells, they finally turned along the path. They started by climbing over the nearest hillock, their first steps towards the unknown…

"Is everything all right?" questioned Stormbright. Only a few moments had passed before Steel halted in his tracks, looking behind them.

The thief turned, now focusing on his brother. "It's nothing," he replied. "I was just thinking that, perhaps in another life, this might have been a good place for us to call home."

Stormbright smiled. "Perhaps it shall be for us, brother. One day…"

They remained silent as they crested another hill, the shadow of the valley covering their tracks behind them.

General Caerst marched across the desolate landscape, along with several dozen soldiers that made up her army. Silence pervaded their number. Their defeat had been so complete, so decisive, that there was no room for excuses.

They had lost the battle against Divnarost—it was as plain and simple as that.

The Falconer felt along her bandaged wounds, noting how close to death she had really come. If it hadn't been for her ingenuity in the end, then she would have certainly shared the fate of her deceased companions.

Who knows? Perhaps she should have died back there…

She cursed, as she would have to make her report to Ilgrathié. It was possible that she might live on from this failure, but regardless, it would come at a cost. In the end, her life only meant so much compared to the greater good of reshaping the world.

However, something about it all felt wrong to her. Their defeat had come mere moments after victory was at hand. And what was more, it seemed like Dimorn had perished within the battle. The demons had turned against them with such quickness, that it made her question how he really died.

Was it possible her adversary's brother was alive, this Stormbright? That would go a long way towards explaining a few things…

She looked above, seeing that the aquamarine heavens were fading into night. The sun was settling fast towards the horizon.

They pitched camp in the looming darkness. The large fire warmed them somewhat, yet even so, there emerged no shred of happiness nor hope. Not a word was spoken among those somber faces. The Ilgrathians consumed their rations, jaws moving slowly, mechanically.

It was some time before General Caerst retreated up a nearby mound, a small copse of trees perched atop it. The scene reminded her of a march she had made a couple years back. That same trek where a young village boy had tried to stab her, before she took them all as slaves…

The realization hit her. It was enough to bring her over the edge. She shrieked out in fury whilst her fists collided with one of the trunks. How could she have been so stupid?! The boy was *him*! *He* had bested her in the end, that little worm! Now she had nothing. Nothing at all. With any luck, Ilgrathié would allow her to live, but at what cost?

Her reputation was ruined.

Emotions taking full hold, she withdrew her rapier and held the edge of it under her neck.

The Falconer froze in place, ready to end her life in a moment's notice. She grimaced, hesitated… before lowering the blade to her side.

"No," she said. "I will not be finished by this. I will not return to Ilgrathié—not until I am through with them. My life is forfeit as it is. I shall make them pay for all the pain, all the humiliation they put me through. Whether it's just one brother or both, I *will* make sure that they are gutted for their crimes! *They will answer to me before the end!!*" She raised her head, looking up towards the skies. "By your will, Your Radiance, I swear to end the lives of Steel and Stormbright! Hear me, O goddess! I shall not rest until they are dealt with. I shall not return until it is done. Once and for all!"

Her voice went still, before she rejoined her companions. A small degree of cheer seemed to return with her not-so-silent prayer. A tiny measure of hope for the days and weeks to come…

Steel & Stormbright
will return!

Glossary

A

Aedas (ay-dus): A human that was captured and conditioned to serve the Ilgrathians, following the realization that he has a talent for astromancy. Aedas acts as an advisor of sorts, as he is one of the few human sorcerers that's allowed to practice his magic. He has thick ebony hair and a somewhat scrawny build.

Aeromancy: The magic school of manipulating winds, clouds, and lightning. Stormbright is an aeromancer himself, although he specializes in lightning.

Alcaron (AL-kuh-RON): The golden empire of Ilgrathié. Alcaron is ground zero for the goddess' vision of Paradise. These lands are wild and teeming with sweet fruits and chirping birds. At least on the surface, it appears like everything one could desire is here; yet there are many dark secrets lurking underneath.

Almari (ahl-MAH-ree): An elite cavalry unit that's been trained to ride rukhs into battle. They are one of Alcaron's main advantages over other kingdoms, as they can fly over city walls with ease. Their weapons of choice are the lance, halberd, and javelin.

Artificer: A type of inventor who harnesses the effects of magic substances, combining them with machinery. Unlike a sorcerer, an artificer has no real control over what kind of magic is produced, save for the innate properties of said materials.

Astromancy: The magic school of peering into the past, present, and possible futures. As one might expect, this talent is highly coveted, as astromancers are quite rare in the world. Aedas and Shariz'lan are both astromancers.

Awakening: When learning the art of sorcery, it is possible to have one's potential awakened in a few different ways: The first is through years of hard work, training, and discipline, whereas the second is being "called" by a powerful entity. Oftentimes this is through a deity, but it can also be achieved by others.

B

Black Tortoise Company: Human mercenary company overseen by Commander Talik. As the name suggests, their company garb is all black.

Bruann (BROO-ann): The second of Zirvonia's two orbiting moons. Bruann is farther out among the skies, though most scholars and sorcerers have agreed that it's the larger of the two.

Brugmar (broog-mahr): A large humanoid beast standing at three-times the height of a regular human. These creatures most resemble a hybrid mix between a lion and a wolf, showing several rows of teeth like a shark. Brugmars are savage beings who are widely feared among Zirvonia. Only the bravest would dare to stand against them.

C

Calamtu (KUH-lam-TOO): The god of storms and fury. Calamtu is a deity to be feared as much as admired, and thus His worship is practiced from afar. He is rarely if ever seen, as He's been spotted only a handful of times throughout the centuries.

Cubit: Measuring unit that's more familiar to ancient history in our world. 1 cubit roughly translates to 1.5 feet, or 0.5 meters.

D

Demon: A type of imp covered in fiendish black scales, with crooked beaks, sharp talons, and tattered wings. Demons are highly-efficient killing machines, even though they're far weaker when divided. Together, however, demons can dispatch even the toughest of prey. They have a penchant for slaughtering in great numbers, and are capable of slaying their allies just as quickly as their enemies.

Divnarost (DIV-nuh-ROST): A once-mighty kingdom that has fallen into ruin over the last century. Nearly all of Divnarost's cities have been overtaken by the curse of the star wraiths, with Miracor serving as the last bastion for the Islirians - the nation's original founders. This is a culture that values omens and knowledge above all else, as they're the very first astromancers to hone their craft.

F

Falcon: The standard Alcaronian soldier. Their garb is either brass or polished moonsteel, with spears and longbows as their preferred weapons.

Falconer: An elite female soldier personally chosen by Ilgrathié, one who's given a drop of the goddess' blood. This grants them enhanced strength, cunning, and dexterity, but does little to alter their appearance. This is one of the highest ranks of Alcaron's military.

Fields of Man, the: A vast series of rolling plains and acacia trees. The Fields of Man is the cradle of human civilization in Zirvonia, one that's given limited autonomy by Alcaron. The lands are shaken by storms that come and go in mere moments, leaving devastation and heavy mudslides in their wake. The Fields of Man serves as an effective buffer between Alcaron and Divnarost, hence why the humans are given a certain amount of freedom.

G

General Caerst (kayrst): An esteemed Falconer, General Caerst is at the head of Alcaron's invasion against Divnarost. She is 47 by the story's conclusion, although by Ilgrathian standards, this is fairly young. She is slim and beautiful. Her eyes are blue and her hair is a vibrant gold, with a long braid stretching down her back.

Geomancy: The magic school of manipulating earth and the forces of nature. Those referred to as druids are often geomancers.

Gladiator Pit, the: An area of the Slave Pits that's much closer to the surface. This is where defiant slaves are given a chance to prove themselves to human mercenary companies. Gamblers and merchants gather from all around, where they wager bets on some of the world's most fearsome fighters and monsters.

Graal (grahl): One of Miracor's many artificers.

Great Beyond, the: A vast realm of seemingly infinite possibilities. The Great Beyond encompasses a host of worlds outside Zirvonia. Under normal circumstances, only trained sorcerers are able to explore these wide, fathomless regions, and even that comes with great risk. It is an ethereal realm, and it's believed that the secrets to life, death, and the meaning of existence may be found here.

Gulizar (goo-lih-zahr): The head shaman of Harskul and brother to Aedas. The man is short, bald, and lanky, with green eyes.

H

Harskul (HAR-skull): The home of Steel, Stormbright, and their father. This is a quaint little village that has an honored history of celebrating the old ways. It is overseen by a shaman, who, by the power of potent narcotics, is able to peer into the future and predict the seasons, along with potential signs and omens.

Heavens Barge, the: An experimental flying ship that resembles a hot air balloon in appearance. There are a number of valves and levers that control its flight, along with a rudimentary wheel steering the fins underneath it. It is four times the height of a regular man, though with its ability to levitate, it is fairly easy to move.

High-Crester, the: The airship of Divnarost's king. The High-Crester takes the form of a massive boat with large fins along the bottom of the stern. Three levitation orbs power it underneath its decks, which allow it to ascend with alarming speed.

Human: A fairly young race in the world, humans first migrated to Zirvonia from the western jungles known as the Obsidian Wilds. For centuries, they have lived in various states of tribal hierarchy. The first major signs of civilization began to develop, yet they were destroyed by the armies of Alcaron. Now they're little more than a subservient race, subjected to their Ilgrathian masters. Humans can live for around 90 years. Their average life expectancy is 25 years.

Human Mercenaries: Once the Fields of Man were conquered by Alcaron, a number of humans escaped and formed their own militia groups. Over time, however, this has turned into a reliable service towards humanity's masters… for a price. When smaller wars and skirmishes are waged, these mercenaries are sent in as expendable assets. The mercenary companies have since brokered a special deal with the Slave Pits, enlisting many of the strongest survivors to their cause.

Hydromancy: The magic school of controlling water, steam, and ice. Ice magic, in particular, is one of the more famous talents in the world. As such, hydromancers are highly coveted.

I

Ilgrathian (eel-GRAY-thee-IN): A race that has existed in the world for several thousand years. The first Ilgrathians were descendants of the people hailing from Kuhstra. Now, they are united under their goddess Ilgrathié. They have light-bronze skin, with hair colors ranging from gold to brunette to steely gray. Even the most normal of Ilgrathians appear like heroes out of legend. That is, until one learns of their lustful appetites. Ilgrathians can live for around 180 years. Their average life expectancy is 60 years.

Ilgrathié (eel-GRAH-thee-AY): The Holy Falcon who will guide the world unto Paradise. Ilgrathié is a pleasure goddess in nature, though Her doctrine requires that the world be cleansed of all other heathen beliefs. Taking its place is nothing short of debauchery. Atrocities such as rape, pillaging, and torture are all permitted, so long as it furthers Her cause. Above all, Ilgrathié's mantra is "pain and pleasure."

Inner Sense: A sorcerer's ability to sense magic. More accurately, it's a way for one to enhance their five senses, detect signs and simulacra that normal beings would likely miss. It should be noted that, over time, this can serve as quite the mental strain.

Islirian (is-LEER-ee-IN): A gray-skinned people who live near the southern edge of the world. Islirians are cursed, doomed to transform into star wraiths upon dying. The only known countermeasure has been to burn the dead shortly before this process can occur. They were once highly respected and feared, but they have since fallen into ruin. Islirians can live around 120 years. Their average life expectancy following their curse is 20 years.

J

Jalkar (jahl-kar): A young Ilgrathian who's a bit overeager for battle.

K

King Telinor (teh-lih-noor): The last monarch of Divnarost before the star wraith curse. Like other star wraiths, he appears like a specter with a starry veil for a body. Only in this case, he wears the old crown of Divnarost, as he holds some air of authority with his subjects.

Kitala (kih-tah-lah): The Queen of Divnarost. Kitala is the youngest ruler since the nation's founding. She is 23 years old by the time she meets the two brothers, although by Islirian years, she is rather close in age to Steel. She has raven black hair, green eyes, and smooth gray skin.

Kolthan (kohl-than): The father of Steel and Stormbright, as well as husband to his deceased wife Tana. Kolthan is a burly giant, with flowing auburn hair, rippling muscles, and a stony demeanor. He is also the chief warrior of Harskul.

M

Miracor (MIH-rah-KOR): The last city of Divnarost that hasn't been overtaken by star wraiths. The Islirians here are a battered and broken people, clinging on to the last vestiges of life. The settlement is in an advanced state of ruin, with much of its knowledge and culture lost to the ages. The city is currently under siege by Alcaron.

Mirungel (MIH-run-GEHL): The capital city of Alcaron. Also referred to by the Ilgrathians as the City of Chimes, Mirungel is the epicenter of all that goes on under Ilgrathié. It is a place that's nestled alongside Aerie Mountain, and here the Ilgrathians indulge in all pleasures imaginable.

Moonsteel: A metal that's nearly ten-times stronger than steel. However, the deposits found in the world are notably rare. Moonsteel is highly valued for its beauty, durability, and tolerance to heat. It can withstand extremely high temperatures, with some claiming that it can even weather a dragon's breath.

N

Necromancy: The magic school of reanimating the dead in order to do one's bidding. This is quite different from the school of sciomancy, primarily because the magician is returning the dead's souls to their bodies. Those who are raised can recall what they went through in life, though they're under the sorcerer's complete control.

Nightmare-Kin: A horrific race of sentient, amorphous monsters bleeding in from the Great Beyond. Unlike other species, nightmare-kin seem bent on the assimilation of all life, morphing their victims into something twisted and otherworldly. Steel and Stormbright encounter a small group of these creatures during their voyage to Talacor.

O

Old Man Darkness: The primeval lord of death and the unknown. Old Man Darkness is believed to rule the infinite realms of the Great Beyond. Even so, very little is known about Him. It's speculated that He created the nightmare-kin, although evidence for this is somewhat lacking.

Oneiromancy: The magic school of warping the laws of physics. Perhaps the most archaic of sorcery, oneiromancers use their power in conjunction with other spells, reshaping the world as they see fit. Whereas most magic is temporary, oneiromancy is permanent. Flying cities among the stars. Volcanoes spewing torrents of liquid ice. Vast underground spaces where the sun shines eternally. All is possible when utilizing this form of magic. The floating island cities of Divnarost are a great example of oneiromancy paired with geomancy.

Oubal (oo-BAHL): A strange spirit hailing from the Underworld, supposedly a remote corner of the Great Beyond. Oubal can change its form at will, though it most often takes the form of a manticore, with a lioness' body, hind hooves of a sow, a scorpion's tail, and a human's face. To a certain extent, Oubal is able to command spirits and even reshape reality. The Realm of the Staff is one such place.

Oubal Staff, the: A priceless artifact created by King Telinor and his sorcerers. The staff can summon and control any manner of spirit from the Great Beyond.

Oun'arc (oohn-ark): A special form of nightmare-kin that can fly through the skies, carrying many smaller abominations upon its massive, wretched form. It is rumored that these are sentinels for even larger creatures, though the evidence for such a theory is inconclusive.

P

Paldar (pahl-dar): A more seasoned Ilgrathian soldier, who is also the father of Jalkar.

Pyromancy: The magic school of harnessing and manipulating fire. Pyromancers are somewhat rare in the world, as most of them don't live for terribly long.

R

Realm of the Staff, the: A small pocket dimension created to imprison Oubal within its staff, although the spirit has since reshaped the realm to fit its own desires. The place is blasted and decrepit, the land blackened and scorched. Fiery flora burn with bright intensity, next to the ash remains of a second species of flower. The sky above is a swirling vortex of crimson, violet, and magenta. At the center of this land is Oubal's domain - a large amber tree that reaches high up towards the heavens.

Rukh (roohk): Large warbird bred by the Ilgrathians, with a wing span of ten-cubits across. They are horrific and aggressive predators, with a fondness for mutilating their prey.

S

Sciomancy: The magic school of summoning spirits from the Great Beyond. Unlike a necromancer, a sciomancer communes with the spirits he commands. One can conjure vast hordes out of thin air, binding them to the sciomancer. Some spirits are more easily controlled than others, and if the magician's focus lapses, then these beings can potentially free themselves and go berserk. Dimorn, for example, is a sciomancer.

Shariz'lan (shar-iz-LAHN): The head chirurgeon of Miracor, as well as the most experienced astromancer of the Islirians. Following the death of Kitala's parents at a young age, Shariz'lan has acted as a guardian for the child. She aids the Queen by gazing into the future, predicting details and possible outcomes of battles. Her appearance is almost hag-like, with a wrinkly face and long, bony fingers.

Slave Pits, the: A series of tunnels and caverns running underneath Mirungel, spanning the different corners of Aerie Mountain. This is a place where humans are beaten and broken: they're whipped, tortured, and defiled so that they might serve the higher castes of society. Only the strong can survive in such a horrific place, as cannibals are allowed to prey on the weak, thinning out a slave population that's already bursting at the seams.

Sorcerers: Also referred to as magicians. Sorcerers in Zirvonia are very powerful. However, they require hard work and discipline to use their magic effectively, even those who are awakened by higher powers. Sorcerers can master only one school of magic, which is based on their personality and talents. It is possible for one to dabble in other schools, though the results are often less than satisfactory.

Soul Cistern, the: A mysterious place where strong souls are taken and extracted. Little is actually known about this section of the Slave Pits, only that it's spoken about in hushed whispers, and with more than a tinge of fear.

Star Crystal: Also referred to as Astrum. A star crystal is an arcane material that's extremely rare in Zirvonia. Exposure to magic can cause it to react in a number of ways, the most notable of which are levitation and concentrated beams of fire.

Star Tower: A tower that's been constructed by Divnarost's sorcerers, primarily as a defense measure for its border cities. Their supercharged beams ward off invaders with ease, toppling siege towers and the like within seconds.

Star Wraith: A strange spectral being somewhat akin to a ghost. Their bodies are like rifts in the fabric of space, displaying starry vistas as if they were a portal to the cosmos. This is what becomes of Islirians following their deaths, assuming their bodies aren't burned.

Steel: Also known as Serithas (seh-rih-thus), Steel is the older of the two main brothers. He is tall and slightly muscular in build, with brunette hair and green eyes. At the story's beginning, he is 15 years old. By its conclusion, he is 17.

Stormbright: Also known as Zolan (zoh-lin), Stormbright is the younger of the two brothers. He has blue eyes and dirty-blond hair flowing down to his shoulders. At the story's beginning, he is 13 years old. By its conclusion, he is 15.

Sutana (SOO-tah-nah): The goddess of night and the heavens. Sutana is widely known for Her introspection and melancholy. Even the stars are said to be Her tears as She weeps for the world below. The Islirians are Her children, and it's believed that they once descended from the stars millennia ago. Following the curse of the star wraiths, many Islirians believe that Sutana has forsaken them. As such, their faith in Her has diminished greatly.

Sylph: A type of spectral fae that glides along the winds, perching themselves atop mountain ranges. It's well known that most sylphs have allied themselves with Ilgrathié, though it's been speculated that a few have defied Her over the years. Sylphs typically emerge from strong gales of wind, and if one is reckless enough to be caught off-guard, they can be torn to shreds in mere seconds.

T

Talacor (TAH-lah-KOR): The capital of Divnarost. It is here that the onslaught of star wraiths is at its strongest. This is where King Telinor once ruled from his high seat, before the nation fell into ruin.

Taldriath (TAHL-dree-ith): The first of Zirvonia's two orbiting moons. Taldriath looms much closer in the heavens. It's believed that, eventually, these celestial bodies will collide and wreak untold devastation on the world.

Trilgar (trill-gahr): An Ilgrathian cutthroat who has been imprisoned in the Slave Pits, following an attempt to ransack his goddess' palace. His appearance is somewhat unorthodox for an Ilgrathian: he has rough, angular facial features giving him the likeness of a rat.

Y

Ya'utet (yah-oo-teht): The head general of Miracor. By the time of meeting Steel and Stormbright, Ya'utet is well-experienced at the age of 48. He has a muscular build, with short-cropped black hair.

Z

Zirvonia (zer-VOH-nee-AH): A wild land inhabited by sylphs, shadow hounds, and other varieties of monsters. In recent centuries, it has been colonized by humans and Ilgrathians, a semblance of order forming over its many plains, rivers, and forests. Still, many ancient secrets lurk in hidden places, hinting at truths far wilder and more fantastic than one could imagine.

A Note from the Author

Thank you, dear reader, for checking out *The Curse of the Star Wraiths*! This has been a passion project of mine for nearly two years, and I hope to bring you more awesome stories featuring the dynamic duo.

If you enjoyed your time while reading, feel free to leave a review on the platform you purchased it. Also, if you're curious about what else I do, I have a blog page where I post short stories, reviews, and the odd opinion piece.

God Bless,
The Lord Otter

Links:

Substack: downstreampulp.substack.com
Twitter: @The_Lord_Otter